D1497652

UNDER ANY
Conditions
Elle Rivers

For those who want more of the couple after their happy
ending. This is for you.

A Note from Elle

This content warning WILL contain spoilers. If you do NOT want to be spoiled and do not need the content warnings, then please skip this page!

This novel does contain: discussions of past alcoholism, discussions of parental abandonment, and includes and on page pregnancy. If these topics are upsetting to you, please take care if you choose to continue this novel. If you feel that this warning is missing any key points, please message me at my Instagram at @elleswrites and I will rectify the situation.

Chapter One

Riley

Being surrounded by weeping parents was not high on Riley's list of favorite places to be.

And it wasn't even like she blamed them. A child's first day of school was hard for any parent. Even she was feeling a little sad to see Zoe grow up.

Her daughter was now entering kindergarten, which meant homework, grades, and new friends. The early learning center Zoe had been in was similar, but this was . . . *bigger*.

Riley felt just as much emotion as any of the other parents did, but she'd rather cry alone in her car than let anyone else witness her tears. The teacher was sympathetic, offering tissues to each emotional parent.

Riley wondered if they would run out by the time the morning bell rang.

"Do you have everything?" she asked as she knelt down to Zoe's height.

"Yes," Zoe answered dutifully. "I have my lunch, my water bottle, and my note from Daddy telling me he loves me."

"You know your dad's proud of you," Riley reminded her.

"Yes," she said confidently. "I know Daddy loves me."

Riley nodded, remembering how Oliver had come home the night before, angry about having to be at work instead of with his daughter on her first day of school. He was afraid Zoe would think he didn't care about her as much as he used to.

Being a CFO was more work than Riley could imagine, and it had only seemed to get busier as the months passed.

Luckily, Zoe wasn't as bothered about it as she used to be.

Riley's mind flashed to the night she met her. The then-smaller child's teary eyes had done a number on her, and she'd taken a piece of Riley's heart that fateful night.

"He said he's sorry," Riley said.

"He has to work. I'm not mad." She shrugged. "He's picking me up though, right?"

"Yes," Riley said. "Right at three."

"Okay," she replied. Other kids were sniffling as their parents left. She eyed them curiously. "The other kids are sad. Should I be sad?"

"Only if you feel like you are."

Zoe frowned, considering it. "I think I'll miss you, but this is like the school I was already in."

"Some kids didn't go to school like you did. So, they're sad and scared. Could you imagine if you hadn't gone before this?"

"Yeah. I'd be sad too."

"Be nice to them, okay?"

"Yes, Mommy."

"Ah, you just be Zoe's mom," the teacher said, smiling, as she approached from behind.

"I am," Riley replied.

"Here you go." The teacher handed her a tissue and Riley realized her eyes had grown wet while talking to Zoe.

She almost didn't want to take it. Teachers already had to pay for too much. They didn't need to be handing out their tissues to moms who promised themselves not to be emotional.

"Thank you." Riley grabbed it just in case she wasn't able to hold back the impending flood. She made a mental note to be sure to donate several Costco-sized packages of tissue boxes in the future. "This isn't all that different than the early learning center she went to before."

"It's a big step, but she's going to be fine. Look at her; she's already socializing!"

Zoe had walked over to another girl who was sniffling at her parent's departure and offered a hug.

"She's sweet," the teacher said, smiling at the scene.

Dammit. Zoe was such a good kid. Seeing her offering kindness rather than judgment only upped the emotion she was feeling. Riley was so damn proud of her.

Could pride cause tears?

Riley replied, "She is." She paused to clear her throat. "I should probably go, though. Looks like she's okay on her own."

"I think that's a good idea. You're doing great." The teacher patted her shoulder and Riley could feel the tears threatening to spill over. She nodded at the teacher and called a "goodbye" to Zoe, who was still cheering up her new friend across the room. Zoe's only response was a wave.

Riley blinked away her tears as she left the classroom; she was proud that she hadn't devolved into actual sobs over this. She'd give herself that win. After passing by one parent in the hallway whose shoulders were shaking as they wept, Riley offered them her unused tissue.

Being a parent was a lot more crying than she ever expected.

Shit, what was she going to do when Zoe *graduated*?

That might break her. She had only known Zoe for a little under a year, but she had changed Riley's life in more ways than one.

And she could only wonder how much more she'd love Zoe years down the road.

Her heart suddenly tightened, and she knew she needed to make a break for the door.

"So, you're Zoe's mom," another parent announced as Riley walked down the hallway.

She paused, turning to face the woman she'd never seen before.

The woman was dressed to the nines, wearing what had to be designer clothes and a diamond bracelet that shined so bright—it probably cost more than Riley's weekly salary.

She dimly remembered this woman from the classroom. She was one of the few parents not crying.

"I am," she said. "Do you know Zoe or something?"

"I live in the neighborhood. Two doors down actually. I have the house with the Jaguar in the driveway."

Riley didn't know much about cars, but she did know that was an expensive one.

"Oh, nice to meet you," Riley said. "I officially moved in about nine months ago." She held out her hand, but it only met air.

"Here's the thing," the woman said, checking out the obscenely shiny diamond ring on her left hand. "I know Oliver. He's never been with the mother of Zoe. He's been single ever since he moved here a few years ago."

"How would you know that?"

"I work for the HOA. We know *everyone*. The only person living there is a nanny that Oliver employs, which I'm assuming is you."

"I used to be Zoe's nanny, yes."

"So, you're not her mom."

"I am," Riley replied, narrowing her eyes. "I adopted her."

The woman slowly walked around Riley, regarding her with a critical eye. "Bold move."

"Bold move for *what*?"

"You know, Oliver has a reputation around there. He's— oh, how do you say it—*sweet*, I suppose. So sweet he never accepts our advances on him."

"Aren't you married?"

"Marriage is a transaction. We go after the highest bidder, and Oliver is very high on that list."

"Oh, come on. He has money, but he's not *your* kind of rich."

The woman laughed. "Oh, you're so innocent. You're lowballing him. You should look up the profits of that healthcare company he runs to really get an idea of how much he and his family are worth. Although, I don't know how you swung *him* when you seem so new to the game."

Riley realized what this woman meant. She thought Riley had gone after Oliver for his money.

"It was pretty easy to swing him, actually. I didn't care about his money and fell in love with him like a normal human being."

The woman frowned. "So, you're not living in that beautiful house? He's never done *anything* for you?"

Riley thought of him covering the adoption fees when she officially adopted Zoe. She'd fought him on it, but he'd won when she saw how much it was going to cost.

Since the start of their relationship, he'd offered to buy her many things. Whether it was a new phone or a new set of pens, she always said no.

But she would be lying if she said it wasn't tempting.

Her pride, however, won over her desires. If she wanted something, she'd be the one to foot the bill, especially since she didn't pay any rent.

Yet somehow, Riley had allowed him to pay for things she couldn't afford.

The woman shook her head. "Oh, you feel *guilty*. Ha! This won't last long." She flipped her hair over her shoulder. "With your looks, I give it three months."

The woman sauntered away, and Riley watched her, fists clenching at her sides. She wanted to yell out all the obscene words she knew, but this was not the place for the f-bomb. So, she settled on something else.

"Hey!" she called. The woman paused but didn't turn. "You have a crayon smear on your backside."

She didn't, but seeing the woman turn in a fruitless effort to find it was more than satisfying.

"I should have had the nanny take the kids to school!" the woman screeched. "This place is disgusting."

By the time Riley spoke again, the other woman was nearly to the building's exit. "Be careful with nannies. I hear they score men out of their league."

The woman went red in the face and barreled outside, ending the conversation. Riley waited until she saw a fancy car leave the parking lot before she followed suit.

Then the words hit her.

How dare she! That woman knew nothing about her, about the struggles she faced in getting where she was.

And yet the words still hurt.

Riley had always wondered *how* she managed to land a man like Oliver. He said he loved her, and she knew he did, but the love didn't make sense. Multiple people had told Riley they didn't match, and she was beginning to wonder if they were right.

After all, she and David had matched.

Look where that got her.

Then again, her relationship with David hadn't survived. And while she wanted to believe that her and Oliver not matching was a good thing—that opposites did attract— sometimes she struggled to.

Pulling off the road into an empty parking lot, Riley opened her phone, planning on playing loud, angry music to scream to on the way home, but the phone instead buzzed with a call.

"Hey, Oliver," she said, trying to get the annoyance out of her voice.

"Is Zoe doing okay?"

"Yeah," she replied as she pulled back onto the road. "She wasn't even upset. She actually comforted some of the other kids in the class."

"That's good. I'm really relieved to hear that. But *you* sound upset."

Riley paused. Of course he would notice she was upset. Oliver was more observant than most of the people she'd known.

"It was an emotional day for me, but somehow not for her."

"I hate that I couldn't be there," he said. "I could kill the new COO for forcing us in today."

Riley had heard a lot about the new COO. He was not hired by Jack or Oliver, but by investors in the company.

Oliver's company was not publicly traded, which allowed them a different kind of control over their finances—as far as Riley knew. They didn't have to get money from stocks like most healthcare companies did, but they did answer to the people who invested in the business. Riley only understood as much as she did because, technically, she was an investor of a company herself.

She could easily persuade Camilla to change everything about her business, but Riley was content only making business decisions that got more people through the door.

"Maybe murder isn't the best option yet," she replied. "Was it that bad?"

Oliver let out a long-suffering sigh. "It was pointless and could have been an email. I really don't like this guy."

It wasn't the first time she'd heard this either. From what Riley had heard from Amanda and Oliver, the new COO was making a lot of big changes—ones that no one was happy with.

"I know," Riley said. "And I know you're mad about not being there today. But she's fine. I think she's excited about school more than anything."

"I'm glad you were there." His voice was soft. "I'm glad I have you."

She blushed and found herself glad she was in her car and not in front of him. Compliments were nice, but they were often hard to accept.

Then she was sidetracked by her left turn, which put the sun right in her eyes. "Ugh," she complained. "I've got to get the front window tinted on this car. The sun is killing my eyes."

"I could—" Someone in the background called for Oliver. "Hey, I have to go. Work calls."

"Okay, have a good one," Riley said. She threw on sunglasses and basked in the relief from the unyielding sun.

He told her he loved her before hanging up the phone. She took a deep breath after the call ended, her mind playing back the woman's words.

Despite how amazing Oliver was, she couldn't shake the feeling she didn't deserve him or his love. When she looked in the mirror, she couldn't find a single thing about herself that a man who deserved a supermodel would be attracted to.

And sure, he said he loved her. But did he feel like he had to? Did he feel like he owed her something for adopting Zoe, for ensuring his little girl would always be taken care of?

When Riley pulled into the driveway, she leaned her head against the steering wheel. She hated it when she thought like this. It broke her heart every time.

It took her a minute to leave the confines of the car. The late summer air was sticky and oppressive. She thought back to when she had walked into David's apartment to find he was with her then best friend.

She sighed. She really was bringing to the surface all of her old traumas in one short morning.

As Riley got out of her car, she glanced over at the other houses in the neighborhood. She'd never thought much of the neighbors because she never truly felt like she belonged in this beautiful area, even after she moved into it.

The woman was totally off base about a lot, but not about one thing: Riley was out of her element, and she didn't know how to go about feeling like she belonged.

Because maybe she didn't.

But Riley didn't have time to think about this. She had to be at the coffee shop for her shift in thirty minutes. She tried to put it out of her mind and get busy.

Oliver

Oliver walked into Zoe's school still fuming about missing her first day.

Executives weren't known for having good work-life balance, but his father had accommodated him on most fronts over the years. He had been able to work from home while he struggled to find childcare for Zoe. He'd been able to work at night rather than during the day when she was a baby and didn't sleep well. While he knew he always had to put in more than forty hours a week, it was flexible in when he did so.

Now, it was a little different.

When Richard, the new COO, had started, it was one meeting after another. Richard didn't believe in using Zoom, and requested everyone involved be there in person, even if it was after five.

He also had the habit of wanting Oliver and Jack in on every single meeting he attended—even if they weren't needed.

This morning's meeting was something neither Jack nor Oliver should have been a part of: an employee complaining about breaks to HR was not CEO- and CFO-level important.

But it was to Richard.

Missing his daughter's first day of school for something so trivial had him furious. If he didn't have Riley, who Zoe loved so much, he didn't know what he would have done.

Zoe was drawing in the corner of the classroom and broke into a grin when he walked in. She ran to hug him and he knelt to catch her.

"Hey, sweetheart," he said. "How did it go?"

"It was fun, Daddy! We learned to count, do ABCs, and learned colors, but Mommy already taught me, so I just watched the other kids."

"Yeah, Mommy got to most of it, didn't she?"

"And the other fun school too."

Oliver smiled at Zoe's mention of her early learning center. That had been another one of Riley's brilliant ideas.

"I'm glad it went well. I'm sorry I couldn't be here."

"It's okay. Mommy was."

Oliver didn't remember how he used to do this alone. Sleepless nights and long days were the easiest of it. Being a parent was so much more than simply *being there*. It meant emotional and physical support. It meant making important decisions for them to help their growth. It meant listening to them after a long day of work. It meant comforting and providing for them when they were sick.

And it had been exhausting.

"You must be Zoe's father," the teacher said. Oliver looked over at her and smiled.

"Yes, I am."

"I met your wife earlier, but I didn't catch you."

"My . . . wife?"

"Yes, Zoe's mom?" the teacher asked. "Unless you two are separated . . . Did you two have different last names? I genuinely can't remember."

"No, we're not separated, but we do have different last names," he corrected. The gears in his brain ground at Riley being called his wife, and yet he was reluctant to correct her.

"Oh, good," the teacher said, "I'd hate to offend. I was honestly so busy this morning I didn't get to talk to her much. Both of them handled it *great* though. Zoe was so attentive in class, and even helped other students who were confused."

"I'd like to say that was all my doing, but it definitely wasn't." That sort of thing had Riley written all over it. She never seemed to see it, but she was one of the kindest people he knew.

"I heard she was in a preschool."

"Yes, Riley planned all of that out. She took care of a lot of this stuff. A lot of it I didn't even realize Zoe was ready for."

"It takes a team," the teacher said. "I don't foresee any issues from here on out, Mr. Brian. I think Zoe will do well here."

Oliver let out a breath of relief, once again thanking his lucky stars he had met Riley when he did, that he had met her period.

He reached his hand out for Zoe's and said, "Come on. Let's go home."

He walked her to the car and buckled her in. Riley had saved him so much grief today. He hadn't felt great about how much he'd been working, and he hated that so much had fallen on Riley's already loaded shoulders. He was so busy that he felt limited in what he could do to help her in return, but there was one area he knew he could do something.

Physical items.

And while he hadn't purchased a gift for her since Christmas, she did seem to like the phone case she received. It hadn't been much to *him*, but it was a nicer one, designed to be both lightweight and very protective. She didn't seem too bothered about it then.

"Mommy really helped me out today. What do you say we make a pit stop and get a treat for her?"

"Yes!" Zoe exclaimed, and Oliver changed his course.

It was five when Oliver got home.

"I want to show Mommy her gift!" Zoe exclaimed.

"Hang on," he said, laughing. "Let me talk to her first. We don't want to overwhelm her the moment we get inside."

Zoe grumbled but agreed.

When they walked in, Riley had just finished her shift at the coffee shop. She had to ask Camilla to cover the first half of the day for her in order to get Zoe to school, and Oliver was so glad her friend was willing to do it.

"Hey," she said, turning to greet them. Zoe gave Riley a hug and told her about her day. Riley listened intently. Once Zoe was content, Oliver brought Riley in for a kiss.

Coming home to kiss Riley was one of his favorite things to do.

He spent his days waiting to see her. He loved her bright smile, reserved only for him and Zoe. He loved her flannels and tank tops, her mind, and her kindness.

She was also one of the most beautiful women he had ever seen.

"Were you late getting her?" Riley asked, glancing at the clock on the wall.

"No, we made a pit stop. She was in a good mood after school today. I was worried she would throw a fit because I wasn't there."

"I think it helped that you came to pick her up, but she seemed fine with it. How did your meetings go?"

Oliver sighed. "Terribly. The COO's new money-saving technique has HR warning us that people aren't taking their breaks. A few people have already quit over it, and one person's exit interview even mentioned a lawyer is getting involved. It could be all talk, but it also might not be."

"And the investors don't see this as a problem?"

"They do. Richard's on thin ice. If there is a lawsuit, we can easily push the blame to him."

"Hopefully then he won't be pulling you to work all the time."

"Exactly," he said, bitterness seeping into his tone. He didn't want to think about work though, so he pushed it out of his mind. He immediately changed the subject. "How was your day?" Her shoulders tightened and he wondered if he'd placed too much on her.

"It . . . it was fine. Just your run-of-the-mill normal day."

Oliver narrowed his eyes at the tense curve of her shoulder. "I doubt that."

"Okay," Riley said, turning back to him. "It was weird. What do you know about the neighbors?"

"More than I'd like. This neighborhood is run by a bunch of moms on the HOA committee. They've tried to get me involved, but I'm not interested."

"I met one of them today at the school."

Oliver could see where this was going. The majority of the women in the neighborhood were the kind that he'd rather stay away from. They all married very wealthy men and immediately had kids in order to achieve the coveted stay-at-home mom title. But when their nannies and maids established order in their homes, the bored housewives took to joining the HOA in order to boss others around in an attempt to keep everything "perfect."

A few of them had tried flirting with him. He'd shut it down immediately.

"Which one?"

"I didn't get a name, but she lives a few houses over from us."

Oliver hadn't kept up with who lived where. He only knew he didn't like talking to them.

"Did she say anything to you?"

Riley bit her lip, not meeting his eyes. He didn't like it when she did this. Usually it meant something bad had actually happened.

"She insinuated that I'm with you for the money."

"She called you a gold digger?"

"Not in those exact words, but . . . yes."

Oliver's chest tensed. Riley was so different from any of those women, so much kinder than they could ever be. She didn't even need to be giving them the time of day.

"What neighbor was this?" He was trying, and failing, to keep his cool.

"Oliver, I don't want to start a whole thing—"

"She insulted you," he said firmly. "That's not okay."

"What are you going to do? Tell her to stop? I doubt I'll even see her again. It didn't seem like the school scene was her thing."

"Riley—"

"I don't need you fighting my battles for me," she said, wanting to put her foot down. "I'm fine. I'm more in shock that she seemed to be under the impression you're the richest man in this neighborhood."

"Why do you say that?"

"I mean, obviously you're well-off. Look at this place." She gestured around the house. "The way she talked, though, it was like you were a multimillionaire or something. Maybe even a billionaire."

"Is it a problem if I was?"

"No," she said immediately. "But you're so . . . down-to-earth. Your car isn't flashy; it's high-end, but still reasonable for a dad to have. This house is nice but there aren't marble sculptures in the foyer or weird, ornamental furniture no one's allowed to sit on. I know that doesn't translate directly, but I guess I never put a number on it."

That was news to him. Most people, especially those who worked with him, knew exactly his net worth. He knew his dad's penthouse had been Googled by employees; his house had been as well.

The company they ran was flourishing, and they did their best to reward their employees for their hard work. People talked, and when they heard their bosses had a lot of money, they wanted to know just how much.

The thing was—Oliver's salary alone wasn't all of his wealth. Some of it was generational, but a lot came from wise investments of his own money. He'd followed in his father's footsteps, and it had worked.

He didn't try to be greedy with it. He donated a lot of the excess money he made to the Second Harvest Food Bank and to various homeless shelters in the area. He also invested in businesses owned by marginalized communities, and many of them had done well.

Hell, he would have invested in Camilla's business had Riley not offered first.

"Oliver?" Riley asked, sounding wary. "This isn't the part where you tell me you're broke and we're selling the house, right?"

"No," he said, shaking his head. "I was just shocked you didn't already know."

"Know what?" Her voice was tense.

"That those people are right."

She blew out a breath and paced around the island. "Really? Like . . . billionaire level?"

"I'm going to be honest: I have no clue. A lot of my money is tied up in investments."

"Oh, that's a rich person phrase."

"Did you really never think about it?"

"I know how expensive this house is. I know you live in Green Hills and that you were able to pay me more than you probably should have, but that number is *way* more than I ever realized. How the hell did you end up with *me*?"

"Well, you took in my daughter as your own and treated me like I didn't have a penny to my name. I think you're beautiful and smart. It was easy to fall in love with you."

Her face broke out into a graceful blush. "I-I mean, thank you, but it still doesn't . . ." She trailed off, eyebrows pulled low on her forehead. "I don't know what I'm thinking."

"Probably that this is different than any previous relationship you've had."

"Yeah, that's somewhat accurate."

"It's the same for me. I'm not used to people who work full-time and aren't after me for my money."

She rolled her eyes. "Apparently, that depends on who you ask."

"You do realize that she did that out of jealousy, right?"

"Yes, but I'm not used to having anything to be jealous of. I didn't realize how catty people can be when they're jealous."

"I'm sorry she was like that to you over being with me," he said, walking to her. "I never want you to feel like you have to defend yourself against others because we're together."

"That's the weird thing. I never actually said we were together—only that I adopted Zoe. She was so mean all because I adopted a kid." She shook her head, arms tightly crossed over her chest.

Oliver knew her feelings for Zoe ran deep. He knew she could take insults about herself because, unfortunately, it sounded like she'd heard them all her life. But ones about her and Zoe? Those were different.

"I seriously doubt she would ever do what you did. Don't ever forgot that *you* adopted her before we were ever together. You didn't do this to get my attention."

Riley's eyes flashed. "Of course not. I would never."

"Then ignore it. What she said means nothing."

"I know." She nodded. She glanced back up at him and smiled. "Thank you."

His eyes were pulled to her upturned lips. Her full-strength grin did unfair things to his stomach. Her gaze on him was like a beam in the night, water during a drought.

Love during loneliness.

"And if you ever need anything, all you have to do is ask."

Riley shook her head. "You know I won't."

"Yeah, I know," he said. "But I like to remind you just in case you forget." Then he remembered his and Zoe's stop on the way home. "By the way, I got you something."

Her lips twisted into a frown. "What? Why?"

"You did a huge favor for me today. It'll make your life easier, promise." He turned to call out to the living room. "Zoe, are you ready?"

"Mommy!" she yelled as she ran into the room. "Daddy got you a gift today." She bounced on the balls of her feet, smiling up at them.

Riley stepped away, hands playing with the bottom flaps of her flannel. "What did you buy?"

She said it exactly like they rehearsed in the car. "We made a special trip to a special store to get you a thank-you gift."

"It really does have a use, and it *will* make things easier for you. Zoe, why don't you go get it?"

Zoe disappeared. Riley's eyes followed her, then returned to Oliver.

"Please tell me it wasn't expensive."

Oliver shrugged. "It wasn't a lot to *me*."

But it was probably too much for her. His new scheme of asking for forgiveness and not permission may not be working out as well as he had hoped.

Zoe ran around the corner with a box in her hands. Oliver immediately grabbed it, knowing he didn't want his sweet, well-meaning, but young daughter dropping it.

"So you had been complaining about your laptop . . ."

Riley's eyes widened. "You didn't . . ."

"It's a computer!" Zoe exclaimed. "For your work!"

Oliver handed her the box. It was top-of-the-line and was more than capable of handling the accounting she did for the coffee shop.

Riley was pale as she took the box. "This is for me?"

"It's a thank-you for all you do."

"The salesman said it had an I-N-T-E- . . . L processor!"

"Very good job remembering that, Zoe," Oliver said.

"T-thank you." It sounded like it pained Riley to say. "How much was this?"

"You don't want me to answer that question."

"I need to pay you back," she said immediately.

"Do you like it, Mommy?" Zoe asked before he could tell her he didn't need her to repay anything; that it was a gift, not a favor. "I told Daddy to get the blue one because you like blue."

"It's very nice, Zoe," Riley said. Zoe looked appeased.

"I'm going to get my doll so she can play on a laptop like Mommy!" Zoe ran off, heading right to her dollhouse.

"I know it might be a lot to you, but your old one can't handle what you do any more. Think about the time you'll save if you're not waiting for it to open spreadsheets and hoping it doesn't crash and you lose all your documents."

"I . . . I don't want to be ungrateful, but I haven't done anything to earn this."

"You didn't seem to mind gifts at Christmas. Did I misread this?"

"You got me a cheap phone case."

"Ah, so you never looked it up."

Riley's eyes widened. She took out her phone to look at it. "*Should* I?"

"It's fine," he said, gently taking the phone out of her hands. "You've taken on almost all the parenting duties since I've been working so much."

"I'm her mother. That's my job. I don't need a reward for doing the right thing."

"And you're right, but it's something that will *help* you. I can't take time off work and help you in any other way, but I can free up some of your time."

Riley looked at the laptop, and then back at him. "It would be nice . . ." She thought for a moment, before she glanced at him again and sighed. "I'm sorry. I *am* grateful. It's just hard for me to accept gifts like this."

"I promise I'm not going to do this all the time." Even if he wanted to. "But this was a special occasion. You've done a lot for me, and for Zoe, this last month."

She opened her mouth to try to argue, but he leveled her with a stern stare. Her eyes darted to the box then back to his face once more.

Sometimes she struggled with the oddest of things, but when he thought about why, it all made sense. She was used to doing everything for everyone and not being thanked for it.

It broke his heart.

"Thank you," she said again. "This really will help."

Oliver smiled and he kissed her on the forehead.

Zoe asked for dinner and Riley headed to the kitchen to feed her, leaving the gift on the couch. He stared at the laptop box. He wished he could do more for her, but even this had seemed to upset her.

And he wanted to give her whatever she wanted. While he always knew she was independent, he also had the desire to treat her to what she deserved, and she deserved everything.

This was so different than any of his previous relationships, but he had long since come to terms with the fact that Riley was *very* different than what he knew.

Chapter Two

Riley

As Riley read the specs of her new, sleek laptop, she wondered how much it must have cost.

Unlike the last gift she had gotten, which was a phone case that *couldn't* have been that expensive, this was huge. And try as she might, she couldn't help but be curious at what something of this magnitude must cost.

When she looked it up, she quickly realized she had made a mistake.

A price with a comma is what she saw, and she nearly fell over.

This was more than one of her paychecks. This was something she couldn't feasibly afford—at least for a long time—if it hadn't been given to her.

How could she accept something she couldn't buy herself? Yes, she wanted it, and yes, it would make her life easier, but she didn't want Oliver to feel like she was incapable of buying things for herself. He didn't have to take care of her. She was fine on her own.

Rubbing her face, she knew she needed to talk to someone. Camilla wasn't working, but Riley knew her best friend was busy with her wife, Vanessa. She almost didn't reach out, but she knew once Camilla found out she was upset and *didn't* text, Riley would be in more trouble.

Riley: So, is there a reason I would be feeling bad that Oliver just got me a very nice gift?

Camilla: Is Zoe in bed? This sounds like a phone conversation.

Riley walked into the office where Oliver still sometimes worked. It had French doors that he closed whenever he was in a meeting. He was currently putting Zoe to sleep, so she knew she would be alone.

Camilla answered on the first ring. "Before you apologize about bugging me, Vanessa is having a nice, lovely bath right now, and I don't feel like being submerged in boiling water to join her."

That made Riley feel slightly better. "You know me so well."

"And even if I wasn't free, Vanessa would get it. I know I'm busier now, but she does also know I have a friend I do like to talk to."

That was also new. Before Sarah became David's other woman, her ex-best friend would try to monopolize her time and often fight with David to get it. She was used to soothing ruffled feathers. Now that everything was fine, she felt like she was petting air.

"Yeah, I know," Riley said. "I'm in a weird headspace."

"Because Oliver got you something?"

"A laptop worth way more than I expected."

"How much?"

When Riley told her the price, Camilla whistled. "Wow, must be a good machine."

"He's been working a lot lately. He said he felt bad about it and wanted to get me something to save me some time. And it will. You know how much I struggle using my old one."

"I believe you once said you hoped it died so you could justify getting a new one."

Riley sighed. "So, why am I feeling bad about this? I know Oliver. He's never once made me feel bad for paying me or for covering Zoe's adoption costs."

"I mean, it's weird having someone treat you, especially when you're not used to it. But also, I haven't heard you say you *don't* want it."

"It's not that, but I feel like I should be able to do this on my own."

"Why?"

"Because . . . Well, depending on people is usually when you get let down."

"Are you depending on Oliver?"

"In some ways. I buy my own groceries, gas, and everything else, but he owns the house. I could never afford this place."

"Right, but you *could* afford a place on your own, and you live there because Zoe's there. I'd say that's more you wanting to be close to Zoe than you depending on him. And even if you were, would Oliver let you down? He's made mistakes, sure, but ever since you two have been together, it's been smooth sailing."

"It has."

So why didn't it feel like it?

"You're fine. Now tell me, what's the laptop like? Is it nice?"

"It's amazing," she replied in an honest, astonished tone. "If I saw someone else with this, I'd be jealous."

"Oliver has good taste."

"Yeah, and we both know I'd never buy myself something this nice."

"See? You get treated and you get something better than you'd get yourself. It sounds like you want this."

"I do," she admitted. "But I wish I didn't."

She could hear Amanda's voice telling her she was getting spoiled. She could hear David saying *he* wanted the nicer thing.

"Are you all right?" Camilla asked. "You sound . . . off."

Riley *felt* off, but she could hear Vanessa calling for her in the background, and she knew she wouldn't be able to give Camilla an answer as to why she felt this way anyway.

"I think I'll be okay. Maybe once I turn on the laptop I'll see why I need it so bad."

"Okay," Camilla said, but she didn't sound convinced. "You'll call me if anything else comes up?"

"Yes," Riley replied, and she already had a list going in her head of things she would probably need to tell her friend.

But she heard Vanessa ask something, and Riley didn't want to take up any more time—especially not after how busy Camilla had been at the shop.

"Are you sure you're good?"

"Yes," Riley said. "I'll be fine. I'll see you at the shop, okay?"

After getting off the phone, she went back to the dining room table to sit with the new laptop. It had been charging, and she opened it to finally turn it on.

The welcome screen came on in an instant.

Her old laptop took five minutes.

This was nicer than any device she'd ever owned. Her phones were always a few years old. She'd never used Bluetooth headphones a day in her life. She didn't even understand the smartwatches everyone wore.

When she was a kid, her mother had enough money to live off of, but they never had extra to spend. Christmases were spent on necessary items. And then as an adult, David wanted to spend all the money on himself. He'd always get the top-of-the-line electronics while Riley quietly saved money in the background for things they would need.

Now, things were different, and she didn't know what to do.

"You have it on," Oliver said as he walked into the kitchen. "It looks nice."

"It's . . . very fast."

"You still sound like you're having a hard time with this."

She looked at her hands folded on the table in front of the computer.

"I promise it's just a gift," he continued. "I don't expect you to do anything in return."

It would almost be easier if he asked her to pay it back.

"I know," she said. "And I *am* grateful."

"You're just not used to it," he said, coming to kiss her on the forehead. "I understand."

Riley clicked through the welcome menu, still struggling to accept it, but coming to terms while Oliver was so close.

"Oh, check this out," he said after a moment. He reached forward and bent the screen backwards. Riley reached to stop him, panicked, but he laughed. "It turns into a tablet."

"They make laptops that do that?"

He smiled over at her. "They have for years."

"Technology is so weird," she muttered. "But . . . I bet it's easier to travel with."

Oliver pressed another kiss to her cheek. "That's what I like to hear."

She nodded, and he told her he needed to get some sleep for the back-to-back meetings he had the next morning. She watched him walk to their shared bedroom before she went to the guest bathroom to splash water on her face.

Then she heard it.

"This won't last long. With your looks, I give it three months."

It was the rude mom from the school. It wasn't said out loud, but her mind played it back for her, an unhelpful recording. Riley's eyes unwillingly traveled down to the mirror.

Brown eyes. Brown hair. She wasn't a model. Her nose was too long. She had a nice smile despite one of her front teeth being slightly crooked. Her oval face was lovely with makeup, and overall, she was pretty, but she looked appalling next to someone of Oliver's standing.

She didn't dress nice. She wore old flannels and tank tops paired with the cheapest jeans she could afford. She had no interest in designer labels or sparkly diamonds.

But Oliver *did* care about some of those things, and she wondered if he wanted her to care about them too.

Once he warmed to her personality, what would be left? People got tired of her the more time they spent with her. Her mother, David, and Amanda all soured on her after a while. Things with Jane had been getting better, but only once she'd moved out of her mother's house and demonstrated she was serious about taking charge of her life, including giving up alcohol and devoting herself to Zoe. And even then, Riley still had to walk on eggshells in her mother's presence.

Riley shook her head and walked out of the bathroom, observing the house around her.

Just a year ago, she'd lived in a dump of an apartment with David, which had old, nearly broken appliances, ratty carpets, and stairs that were death traps.

Now she lived in a near mansion.

Oliver's house was massive. It was a two-story brick house nestled on top of a hill in a gated community. The security guard *still* gave her weird looks when she presented her resident's card. She hadn't dared to go to the community pool.

The inside of the house was more than she could ever dream of. Vaulted ceilings, a huge kitchen with marble countertops, and real wooden flooring throughout.

This was beyond what her mother ever had. This was beyond what she ever thought *she* could have.

And sometimes, she wondered if she *did* have it.

Riley wasn't good at this. She wasn't elegant or perfect. She was only herself and could never be anything different. She was terrified that one day Oliver would look at his life, look at *her*, and regret getting involved. Maybe one day his eyes would wander and he'd find someone prettier than she could ever be.

It was becoming one of her worst fears.

She'd always have Zoe. That much she could be sure of. Her lawyer assured her the adoption couldn't be taken back. If Oliver ever found someone else, at least she wouldn't lose the little girl she cherished more than anything.

But she could easily lose him.

Riley fell in love with him a little more every day, and as that happened, she knew the pain of him leaving would become worse and worse. She was getting attached, so much so that she couldn't imagine being single again. She couldn't imagine *looking* at someone else, not when Oliver had her heart.

But did he feel the same way?

It wasn't that she didn't trust him. No, it was that she didn't *blame* him. Other women were interested—other women who looked way better than she ever could.

David hadn't been the one for her, but he had still cheated on her; if someone supposedly so matched with her could stray, what was keeping Oliver? He was way better than David in every aspect, but she still didn't understand why he chose *her*. Why not someone else?

She sighed. She hated how much time she wasted thinking about how it all would end, but she didn't know how to stop.

God, she loved Oliver.

And she was terrified that it would end like most of the love she'd ever known.

Oliver

When Oliver woke up the next morning, he could only think about one thing:

Zoe's teacher calling Riley his *wife*.

He'd been thinking about putting it to paper for a while, but hearing it said out loud only made him want to do it more.

He wanted to be her husband.

He also wanted to see her before he started his day.

Since they'd started dating, Oliver tried to stop by Riley's shop regularly both to visit and to get coffee. Camilla's coffee was delicious, but there was something about seeing one of his favorite people while he got an excellent drink that made him want to continually return.

Riley was behind the counter, working on something with an adorable frown plastered across her lips. He smiled when he saw her, even though he'd already seen her before she walked out the door on her way to work.

She glanced up, frown turning into a smile of her own. "Hey. Want your usual?"

"I'm thinking about mixing it up today. Maybe a latte."

Riley faked a gasp with a hand shooting to cover her mouth. "Who are you and what have you done with my boyfriend?"

He laughed as she turned to work on his order.

"I can pay this time."

She rolled her eyes. "Shut up. You're not paying."

He didn't disagree with her but took note on the way she refused to accept no for an answer. She'd always been like this when he came in, and he wondered if the same method would work on her when he inevitably wanted to get her another gift. Her birthday was right around the corner, after all.

While she made the drink, Oliver glanced around the coffee shop. They weren't slow. Customers filled almost every table. He turned back to her, and she was already holding out the drink for him. His eyes were caught by her ringless hand.

"There you go. A vanilla latte for my favorite customer."

"You just guessed I wanted vanilla?"

"Was I wrong?"

She wasn't.

"One of these days, I'm going to surprise you and get caramel."

"That will be the day the world ends. You hate caramel."

He smirked before taking a sip of the drink.

"So," Riley said as she wiped the espresso machine's steam wand with a damp rag, "any news or did you just come here to flirt?"

"A little of both. I . . . think I'm going to be late coming home today."

"Another late meeting?"

"Something like that," he replied. "Will you be okay to pick up Zoe?"

"Yeah, I get off at two."

"Sounds good." He hesitated a moment. "Would it be too unprofessional to ask for a kiss?"

She laughed and walked around to the front, kissing him goodbye.

He couldn't wait for the day to be over so he could take another step toward asking her to marry him.

After his workday was over, he stopped by a jewelry store. He'd been here before when shopping for a ring for Sophie, but that never came to fruition. Even when he was so sure he could ask that kind of woman to marry him, he never actually took the plunge.

Oliver supposed a part of him always knew it wasn't right.

It wasn't like that this time. He was sure, and if he found the right one, then he would buy it immediately.

Different rings shone in the bright lights of the store. He stared at them all, wondering which one he could see on Riley's finger.

"Can I help you?" a woman asked from behind the counter.

"Yeah," he said. "I'm wanting to ask my girlfriend to marry me. I need a ring."

"Congratulations!" she said, smiling. "What's your budget?"

"No budget. I just need something that suits her."

"Okay. Follow me. I have a few to show you."

She led him to a section of rings that were all sparkle. Many had large diamonds and shined so much they almost hurt to look at. She pulled out a tray to show him, and he was tempted by a few, but his goal was to pick something not only he liked—but Riley too.

She was not flashy. She still wore her flannels, and he had yet to see her in a dress. All of these rings were gorgeous, but he couldn't see any of them on her finger.

Even the less flashy ones—the diamond solitaires—didn't suit her. If he was doing this, then he would do it right.

And none of these were right.

The saleswoman noticed his indecision and gave him a pamphlet of rings they could order. He made a mental note to hide this in his drawer so Riley wouldn't find it.

He left, feeling disappointed he didn't see anything that was perfect. He knew Riley, but this was a ring she would, hopefully, wear for a very long time. He wanted her to love it.

And there was no way he could ask Riley what she would like without her figuring out what he was doing. If she did figure it out, he wouldn't be surprised if she tried to talk him out of buying it and tried to buy it herself, or insisted she didn't need one.

He knew he'd have to keep looking whenever he had free time, which was not as often as he liked.

When he arrived at the house, Riley was in the dining room. She had both old and new laptops on the table in front of her, looking focused. Zoe watched a movie in the background.

Oliver said hello to his daughter first, then he ventured over to Riley.

"What are you up to?" he asked, kissing her forehead.

"Partially working, but also transferring all my files to the new laptop." She looked at him and smiled. "It's way faster than the old one. I needed an upgrade."

"I knew it would help."

"But I could have—"

"I know you could have done it, but I also know you wouldn't have. You'd rather get something for Zoe instead."

She sighed. "Okay, maybe that's true. I'm sorry I'm weird about gifts. I'm just not used to . . . being valued."

There were times Oliver wished he could punch her ex for how he treated her.

"You'll get used to it," he said.

She smiled, but he could see the haunted look in her eyes like he always did when she was thinking about the past. He wished he could take that from her. Oliver knew her pain wouldn't disappear overnight, but he hoped he was better than the men of her past.

And even if it took years to get that look out of her eyes, he would be next to her for all of it. This was how he knew she was the one. He would do anything for her, if only she would let him.

Chapter Three

Riley

Riley wasn't sure where she and Amanda stood, and each day was different.

Nine months ago at Jane's Christmas dinner, Amanda's husband accused her of cheating on him with Oliver. Two months later was when Riley and Oliver officially started dating, and now, three months had passed since Amanda had decided to get divorced. Riley's sister looked more tired than ever. Riley had long since realized Amanda's life wasn't perfect, and she had rushed into marriage and kids to make it look like it was. James was never a supportive husband, and she'd hated him for it.

Thankfully, Amanda was doing well for herself since Oliver negotiated a new position for her at the office. It paid more, which meant Amanda was able to support herself while going through the motions of divorce.

And one of those motions was cleaning out all of the things James left behind in the house.

It was a Tuesday, and Riley had offered to help despite being tired from working at the coffee shop all day.

Zoe was busy with Luke and Landon. Since she had gotten over her fear of the boys, they had all become good friends. They all went to different schools, and Zoe had taken to calling them her cousins and asking to see them at least once a week.

It gave Riley a reason to see Amanda and help her out with the mess James had left behind.

"Son of a bitch," Amanda said under her breath. She pulled out four boxes from the back of the bedroom closet. "He shouldn't have left this much when he moved out."

"Seems like he enjoys half-assing things," Riley answered as she opened the box. "It's all going to Goodwill, right?"

"Yeah," Amanda said. "He's not getting any of this back. If it was important to him, he should have taken it with him."

"Are you okay?" Riley asked. Amanda raised her eyebrows. "I mean, I know you're not, but how are you really doing?"

Amanda sighed. "It's . . . I'm fine. I don't miss being married. Sometimes I felt like he was more of a child than my own kids are. I have one less mess to clean up. But . . . it is lonely."

"He sounds like a loser, but even we miss those sometimes."

"Now I get why you were sad about David, and James didn't even cheat." Amanda sat on her bed, looking upset. "But it's the right thing to do. Luke and Landon didn't need to see him treat me like that. What kind of role model is that?"

"I definitely think it was right, and the loneliness doesn't last forever."

"Easy for you to say. You ended up with the king of all men."

Riley felt the familiar sinking feeling in her gut whenever someone talked about how perfect Oliver was.

"Maybe," she said. "But it wasn't easy."

Sometimes it still wasn't.

"You still ended up with him," Amanda said, throwing some of the old clothes into a garbage bag. "You should let him buy you a new wardrobe or something."

"I . . . couldn't."

"You're missing out. Have you seen the suits he wears? His closet is worth more than your car. He'd probably get you some amazing things."

Her mind flashed to the expensive, but comfortable, shoes she'd been wanting for work. Would Oliver buy those for her if she asked?

Then she cringed.

No. She was not going to ask that of him. She could do this herself.

"Maybe." Riley wanted to change the subject. *Fast.*

"He's so amazing. I sometimes wonder if things would have been different if I had gotten divorced sooner. Hell, maybe *I* would have ended up with Oliver. He was obviously the better guy."

Riley froze. She was no stranger to hearing that Amanda was the better of the two of them. Many people had called her prettier and more put together. Her sister never had as bad of a drinking problem, and she had a regular nine-to-five job. Amanda's accomplishments always outshone Riley's.

Maybe Oliver *should* have ended up with her.

Riley blinked, feeling her eyes grow wet as she thought about it. This was the last thing she needed on her mind after how dark her thoughts had gotten over the last few days.

"Riley, you okay?" Amanda asked.

"Um, yeah," she said, clearing her throat. "I guess I was the lucky one."

"For real." Amanda's voice hardened, turning into a bitter tone Riley was growing familiar with.

Thankfully, she didn't have to hear it much longer because Zoe ran in, asking for something to drink.

Riley was quiet for the rest of her visit with her sister. She finished what she said she would do, and then got the hell out of there. Amanda didn't even notice her sister's sullen mood past the one time she asked.

Once back at the house, when Riley saw Oliver's car, she wondered what he was even doing being with her. He deserved so much *more*.

"Can we play dragons?" Zoe asked after a moment.

Riley forced her thoughts away.

"Of course."

Grateful for the distraction, Riley went inside and played with her daughter. Oliver was working on something in his office and didn't come out until a few minutes after they walked through the front door.

"How did it go at your sister's house?" Oliver asked.

"She was Amanda," Riley replied. "Blunt as always."

"Did she say anything to you?"

Riley considered telling him. And maybe she should have.

But she didn't want to put the idea in Oliver's head. Maybe, deep down, he did have some feelings for Amanda. Maybe her saying it would set it into motion. Maybe it would even start a fight if she didn't bring it up in the right way.

There were too many ways this could go wrong. There was no way she could bring it up.

"She's just upset about her divorce, as usual."

"I think any of us would be," he replied.

Riley opened her mouth to answer, but her phone jingled. It was a text from an automated number, telling her that she was due for her annual checkup at the gynecologist, and she should come in if she needed to make any changes to her birth control.

She knew she needed to make an appointment. She was terrible at taking her birth control regularly. There were many times she was worried her period wouldn't come.

Considering she and Oliver hadn't even talked about more kids yet, she needed to get it figured out.

"I need to go do something," Riley said. "Zoe, are you okay if I leave?"

"Can Daddy play?"

"Sure," Oliver said. "Is everything okay?"

"It's nothing serious. I need to make an appointment with my gynecologist for my annual."

"What's that?" Zoe asked.

"It's a doctor for ladies. You'll have to go when you're older."

"Ew," Zoe said, scrunching her nose.

"I'll be back in a few."

Riley excused herself to make the appointment. The office was closed at such a late hour, but she was able to schedule one online.

It took far longer than she wanted it to, but once it was done, she knew it was the right move. She was so busy that taking a pill every day simply slipped off her radar. The last thing she needed was to add a surprise baby to their already chaotic life.

Oliver

"Is everything okay?" Oliver asked.

Riley came back into the living room fifteen minutes after stepping away. She looked tired, and Oliver feared her day hadn't been good.

"It's fine. I'm thinking about switching my birth control. I forgot to take it today. *Again*."

"Really?"

"Yeah, and now that I'm seeing someone who doesn't care about his video games more than me, I should probably be on something I can remember to regularly take."

Oliver had never had to think about this kind of thing before. He wished there was something he could do other than only condoms. He would use one, but he'd figured out very quickly that he and Riley enjoyed *not* using one.

"It's a good time to talk to my doctor about it," she continued. "We don't want an accidental pregnancy."

"Right."

"I mean . . ." She glanced at him nervously. "We haven't talked about kids, but at least you have practice with it."

His chest tightened. "Oh no. I don't think I can do it again."

"An accidental pregnancy? Or kids in general?"

"Kids," he replied. "Zoe was a nightmare. I love her to death, but the first year was a blur. I think it ruined any future kids for me."

"Really? So . . . you don't want more kids? Like ever?"

He could hear the disappointment in her voice. He almost wanted to lie to her and take it back, but he couldn't—not about this.

"Probably not," he replied. "I wish I could say I would change my mind, but I'm not sure I will."

Riley's shoulders fell, and he hated that it was him who had caused it.

"That's fair," she replied eventually, despite seeming so disappointed. "I can't imagine what you went through raising her on your own. We can always discuss it later."

Oliver's relief was palpable. This was one of the things he loved about her—she was so understanding.

"Thank you," he said.

"You don't have to thank me," she said. "It's human decency."

"That's in short supply."

"Yeah, you're right. Did I tell you about the lady who threw a coffee cup at one of my baristas? Absolutely awful behavior."

"What the hell?" Oliver asked. "Was anyone hurt?"

"It was an empty to-go cup, so no. I kicked her out though. Maybe I should start a wall of shitty customers who are banned from coming in."

He laughed. "Maybe you could have that writer's group you invited write some dramatic stories about them and set them up in a rack for free by the door."

"It could be what differentiates us from the competition," she said, smiling.

"There's that smile I love." He walked over to kiss her. "I missed that."

"Yeah," she said, blushing. "Sorry if I've been in a weird mood."

"You were with Amanda. It's always a risk." At Riley's confused look, he added, "She's not a bad person, but she knows exactly what to say to push your buttons."

"That's an understatement," she muttered.

"I never really talked about personal things when she worked for me, but when I hired you, I started to see it."

"Really?"

"Yeah, she has a knack for always finding the worst thing to say."

"She kind of does," Riley admitted. "I'm glad you said it. I was feeling like a bad sister for thinking it."

"I don't think you could be. After all, you did go and help her clean her house today after working at the shop."

"Careful, Oliver," she said. "I might start getting a big head."

"You? Never."

Although he might like it if she did. There were many times Oliver wished she was more confident in herself. He sometimes hated how much her family, ex, and even he had made her feel less than what she was.

But he was making it his personal mission to make her feel better.

Oliver kissed her, relishing her lips on his. He pulled her in by the small of her back, her body flush with his.

"Why don't we go to bed for the night?" he suggested. "You're tired and I think we both could use some rest. I can put Zoe to bed."

She nodded, and headed to the bedroom. After Zoe was tucked soundly into her bed, he followed.

There was a part of him that wanted to kiss her more—to feel her body against his and have her come apart underneath him.

But she was asleep the moment her head hit the pillow. He watched her sleeping face, knowing she was under some kind of stress she wasn't sharing with him. Her eyes were tired and distant through the day, and he hoped that her getting some rest would help.

He turned off the lights and laid next to her, pulling her back against him. He inhaled her lovely scent and felt himself drift off to sleep too.

Chapter Four

Riley

There was something so humbling about sitting in an office with only a thin sheet covering your bare ass.

Riley hated going to the gynecologist. Then again, she didn't know of many people who liked it.

Luckily, she only had to be in a state of undress for a few minutes before she could leave. Her routine and preventative testing weren't terrible to have done, but it wouldn't be too comfortable either.

The doctor was quick about it. As soon as everything was finished, she was allowed to get dressed before her doctor returned to finish up the appointment.

"Thanks again for coming in," the doctor said. "So, how is the birth control you're on working for you?"

"Um, it isn't. I'm a little too busy with my child and full-time job, so I keep forgetting it."

"A child?" The doctor frowned and looked at her chart. "We didn't have a pregnancy in your chart."

"No, my daughter isn't biological. I adopted her."

She tensed, waiting for the myriad of questions. Some people took it well, and others seemed to consider her not really a mother for not giving birth to her child. Her mind flashed to the woman at the school and her heart sank.

"Oh," the doctor said, smiling. "I can see how your schedule filled up then. How about we discuss options that are a little easier to be consistent with?"

Riley felt her chest loosen. Thank God there wasn't a comment about her adopting Zoe. That would have been the icing on the cake of her shitty week.

"Yes," Riley replied. "I'd love that."

The doctor nodded, going over the few options she had. Riley could choose from two different implants—one in her arm or one in her uterus. The second option was something Amanda had done and apparently it had *hurt*. And if Amanda said it hurt, then it definitely did. She'd had her first child without any pain management, after all.

In telling the doctor she'd go with the arm implant, her doctor explained they would have to wait for it to come in. They also could only put it in at the beginning of her cycle if they wanted it to work immediately. Riley did get a refill of her current birth control, but she wondered if she would even remember to take it.

"Now, I want to remind you," the doctor started as Riley grabbed her purse, "it takes two weeks of consistent use for the pill to really be in your system. So, if you miss it, use other protection."

Riley nodded absentmindedly, thinking about how she was going to manage picking up the prescription in her already busy schedule.

She left the office feeling no more put together than when she came. It had been a long day already, but thankfully she was set to see Camilla for the first time in weeks. A new manager had started, and Riley had pushed their paperwork through as soon as possible to get them hired and trained. Camilla now had more free time.

They were meeting at a smoothie place downtown. It was close to her doctor's office, and they could walk the park and catch up.

"Riley!" Camilla exclaimed, hugging her the moment she saw her. "It's been so long since I've seen you. I mean, we've talked on the phone, but it's *so* not the same."

"I'm sorry," Riley said.

"As if it's your fault," Camilla replied, waving her hand dismissively. "Let's get smoothies. I'm dying for something cold in this heat."

After they ordered and received their drinks, Camilla led them to Centennial Park. It was warm, but not hot. Riley had a few hours until she needed to pick up Zoe from school.

"So, what's been up?" Camilla asked.

"You first."

"Nothing much has happened with me. I can tell just by looking at you something's up, though."

"You can?"

"Oh yeah. You get this sad look in your eyes. Who do I need to kill?"

"No one," Riley said. "Maybe this mom from Zoe's school, and Amanda, and . . ."

"Let's start with the mom."

"She called me a gold digger."

"Holy fuck, she *what?*"

"Yeah. Apparently she lives two houses over and tried to hit on Oliver because he's, you know, rich. Like multimillionaire rich."

"Yeah, obviously."

"Isn't it . . . weird? That he's so rich?"

"No." Camilla shook her head. "I'll admit, I looked him up when he came into the coffee shop in an Armani suit."

"What is an *Armani* suit?"

Camilla stared at her in bewilderment before she laughed. "Do you really not know designer names?"

"Why would I know that? My idea of designer is going to American Eagle once in a blue moon, and even then, on a sales weekend."

"Oh, Riley. Never change."

"I'm not," she said, her face red. "Is it bad that I don't know?"

"Of course not."

"I mean, those suits are expensive, right?"

"Very."

Anxiety shot through her. "All of this money—people make it sound like a status symbol."

"To some, it is."

Riley frowned.

"Does him being rich bother you?" Camilla immediately noticed her change in expression.

"No . . . Yes . . . Maybe."

"Why?"

"Because he's way better off than me. I feel like I provide nothing."

"Do you have to provide anything?"

"Of course I do. I can't depend on him."

"Why not?"

"Because then I'd be in trouble when he eventually leaves me."

Camilla's eyes widened, and Riley tried to tack on an awkward laugh, hoping Camilla would think she was joking.

"Are you okay?"

"Yeah, of course."

"Like, seriously."

"I'm fine," Riley said. When Camilla leveled her with a stern look, she added, "I think."

"I don't think you are. What's really going on?"

She opened her mouth to reassure her that everything was fine, but Camilla's stare was serious.

"I don't know," Riley said. "But I don't feel like myself. No one's done anything. Oliver has been great. He's attentive and kind and understanding. There's nothing wrong."

"But you don't feel like yourself."

Riley sighed. "No."

It was hard to admit, and she wondered if Camilla would tell her she was being ridiculous. There really wasn't anything going on, so in theory, she *should* be fine.

"I'm sorry Riley. Have you talked to a therapist about this?"

"What? Why would I need therapy?"

"Therapy is for everyone."

"Therapy is for people with real problems."

"Your problems are real, Riley."

"Not in comparison to the other things people face. I mean, Amanda is getting divorced. My mom was left by my alcoholic dad, and neither of them needed therapy."

"Yeah and look at how they turned out. Amanda still talks down to you and your mom just now admitted you were your sister's equal. That's not normal. They could have benefitted from it. Hell, maybe they should look into it too."

Riley paused.

"Also," Camilla continued, "you were cheated on. Your mom favored Amanda over you for years. That does damage."

"It wasn't that bad."

"Did it hurt?"

Riley wanted to say no, but that would be a lie. She knew better than to think that Camilla would take anything but the truth.

"Of course it did. All of it did."

"All pain is real, Riley. Sure, you're in a better place *now*, but what happened in the past can still affect you for years.

From what you've said, it's like you're waiting for things to fall apart, even though you don't have to."

Riley had nothing to say, because Camilla was right.

"You stopped drinking on your own," she added. "That was amazing, but you're still *hurting*. Why not talk to a professional about these things? Let them decide if you need to be there."

"And what if they say I don't need it?"

"Honestly, I doubt they will, and if they do, then I'd say get a second opinion. I used to go to one, and I really liked the office I went to. You could try going there."

"You've been to therapy?"

"Of course I have. Almost everyone has—except the women of your family, apparently. When my family cut me off for being with a woman, I had to go."

"I understand. I mean, that is something *serious*—"

"And what you're going through is just as serious. One person's tragedy is not the barometer to measure yours against."

Riley thought about it, but Camilla's no-nonsense stare told her she needed to listen.

"What do I do? Just call them?"

"Yes, that's all you do. You've got this."

Riley nodded, and Camilla gave her the number to the office. She felt guilty, like she didn't need help, but the concern in her friend's voice made her at least want to give it a try.

Maybe this was the right thing to do. Maybe talking to someone could help, if they thought she had enough wrong to warrant it.

Riley called later that day, and after setting up an appointment, she went to add it to the calendar she shared with Oliver.

She stopped before she did, though.

Therapy was something no one talked about in her family. And while she *hoped* Oliver would be open to it, as he was for so many other things, she wondered if this was somehow different.

No one she knew, other than Camilla, ever talked about therapy.

What if doing this made him question her? Made him think she was more broken than she was?

She didn't want this to be the catalyst to their end. Maybe she needed to talk to the person before she brought Oliver into it. If they thought she needed it, then she would tell him.

Oliver

"Are you serious?" Oliver asked, frustrated.

"Yes," Richard said. "The courts took the case."

Oliver had a headache. Richard was leaning back, as if he wasn't bothered by the fact that their company was now in a public lawsuit.

"Why didn't she take breaks?" Jack asked, frowning. "Was it because of the new policies you implemented?"

"No chance. She probably forgot and is now suing *us* because of her own failure."

Oliver glared. It didn't matter who was right or wrong. As an employer, he believed they were tasked with protecting their employees. Richard had only been hired because of his proven money-saving ideas. These must have been what they were.

But Oliver's company wasn't bankrupt. It was far from it.

A recession loomed, however, and investors wanted Richard to cut costs.

So far, their turnover rate had doubled, and Oliver had been working twice as much to get the same amount of work done. No one was happy, and the company felt further away from what he and Jack had ever wanted.

"It's our job to ensure our employees have mandated breaks," Oliver said. "What was your new policy?"

"Employees must be *seated* at their desk for eight hours of the day."

"That sounds illegal," Oliver replied.

"It's not," Richard corrected. "I never told them *not* to take breaks. I've used this policy at many companies before. The difference was that those employees knew how to respect management. You allowed your employees to get entitled with your fancy benefit packages and lackluster break policy.

Jack's eyes met Oliver's, the disgust evident.

"Nevertheless," Richard continued, "I have it covered. Legal is all over it. They're making sure all employees know they must take breaks or risk being fired—"

"That's a strong policy," Oliver interrupted.

"It's what's needed to ensure no one does this again," Richard added sternly. "We're proving our innocence and her negligence. But we'll need detailed hours-logged records of each employee. I believe that's your department, Oliver."

It was only his department because the head of HR had quit. Now they only had Steph, the director, and she was just as busy as he was.

"I can't get that done," he said. "I don't have the time or the manpower."

"This *is* an unrealistic request," Jack added.

"I already thought of that," Richard said. "I found a girl in legal, some blonde who's eager to assist you."

Oliver froze. A blonde in legal?

No.

"Hang on," Richard said, typing on his computer. "I'll IM her to come and introduce herself."

Oliver glanced at his father, trying to convey how bad this could be. Jack knew what this person had done to Zoe, and he wasn't sure he could take seeing her again, even in a professional setting.

Oliver hadn't gone down to the legal floor in months because he didn't want to see her. Amanda knew not to let her in, and he had her blocked on everything. If he did see her, he fixed her with a cold enough glare to scare her away.

Now he might be *working* with her?

"You called me?"

Oliver looked at the door, and there she was—Sophie.

She was playing innocent today. She was all smiles, just like the day he met her. He used to think she was beautiful, but now knowing what was in her heart, he couldn't have found her any more unattractive. He wanted nothing to do with her.

He preferred brunettes that didn't hurt his daughter, anyway.

"Yes, Sophie," Richard said. "You'll help Oliver with this special project."

Sophie's eyes moved to his. She smiled again. "I can do that."

"Hang on," Jack said. "These two dated. It's not professional—"

"Professional? What—Oliver can't work with an ex?"

"No," he said through gritted teeth. "I can't."

"Well," Richard said, leaning back again, "if *you* are willing to explain to the investors why we lost this case, then sure. You can bow out."

"That's not necessary, Richard. How about *you* facilitate what is needed from Sophie? It will give them space, and the project can get done."

Oliver wasn't happy. But he would do it.

"Fine." Richard looked annoyed. "I'll play messenger to you. Happy?"

"No," Oliver said.

"I am," Sophie said. "I think we can work well together."

Oliver shook his head. The meeting adjourned a few minutes later, but Sophie's eyes stayed on his. He tried to ignore her, but she was persistent.

He tried to get out of there as quickly as possible, but she caught up to him.

"Oliver!" she called. He paused, turning only when he noticed people were looking. He knew many had found out they dated last year, and considering his position as a boss, he knew he had to be careful how he interacted with her if he wanted to keep his reputation intact. She smiled when she saw him. To most, it would be a friendly or grateful gesture, but now that he had seen her true colors, he knew it was anything but.

"What?" His voice came out low.

"I wanted to apologize for what happened to Zoe. I never got to because of that *nanny*, but you and I both know I was new to kids, and it makes sense I would falter when learning how to be a parent."

"You were never Zoe's parent," he said firmly.

"I could have been."

Oh, how he hated being reminded of that. Looking back, getting with Sophie was one of the worst decisions of his life. He was forever grateful to Riley for pulling him out of that terrible headspace.

"And now you're not. If I didn't make it clear, you will *never* see her again after what you did to her."

"I didn't mean to hurt her, and I didn't. But I laid down the law. She was walking all over you."

"Lay down the law? There's a huge difference between setting boundaries and what you did, Sophie. I'm not forgiving you for this."

"She pushed *me*, Oliver."

"Zoe isn't physical."

"She pushed me mentally. You and I know mental health is real too."

Oliver looked at her incredulously. She held firm.

"We're not doing this. I'm not happy you're on this project with me, and you've been instructed to deal with Richard, not me."

"I know you're lonely, Oliver," Sophie said in what she thought was a kind, calm voice. It grated on his nerves.

"I'm not lonely," he said, and this time it was the truth. "Stay in line, Sophie. I will get you kicked off this project if you go too far."

"I think I hear some deflection," she said smugly.

Oliver walked away. He didn't want to talk about his personal life at work, and he especially didn't want to talk to her.

Not many people, other than Amanda, knew he was even dating Riley. It wasn't that he was ashamed of her or had anything to hide, but he was in a high-level position at work. He didn't want to be a part of the streams of gossip when people found out he was now dating his old nanny.

He wondered if any of them would want to fill the position as his dating partner, considering his standing at the company.

He had sidestepped when dating Sophie because of his own desperation not to be alone, and never directly dealing with her in the office. Even so, he told her to keep it under wraps, but he doubted she did once he had broken it off and she was kicked from his life. Oliver had hoped she would quit and find some other gullible person to prey on.

It didn't seem like he had much luck in that department.

He tiredly rubbed a hand on his face. His ex's resurgence into his life was a problem, one that would be around for a while. He needed to tell Riley before it caused any issues.

But he had a distinct feeling she was going to hate this.

Riley was playing with Zoe when he walked in. While she always seemed to smile brightly at Zoe, he could see her exhaustion when Zoe was turned away.

He hated that he had to bring up something like this when she didn't seem like herself. He didn't want to make anything worse for one of the most important people in his life.

But there was no option not to tell her.

Oliver wouldn't lie—he'd thought about not even mentioning it—but he knew Riley, knew that she was smart, and she would figure it out eventually.

And if he didn't tell her, a secret like this would be a betrayal—too close to what David did. Oliver doubted Riley knew, but he saw how she looked at him. Usually, it was the full brightness of her smile, with both corners of her lips upturned, one that traveled to her eyes and added a beautiful twinkle to her brown gaze. But sometimes it was with a worried expression, like she was waiting for the other shoe to drop, waiting on him to hurt her like everyone else had.

And now, he had the chance to.

But he never would.

Not that he even could. Riley noticed his irritated mood the moment he walked in. She knew his work was stressful sometimes, but this was more than the usual amount.

"Is everything okay?" she asked as they cooked dinner. Zoe was on the other side of the kitchen, pretending to cook like they were.

"We can talk about it later," he told her. "This isn't something that should be said in front of Zoe."

Both he and Riley followed the unspoken rule to never mention Sophie in front of Zoe. Oliver had mentioned the very few times he had seen her at work to Riley, and Riley only. He'd messed up once by introducing Sophie into their lives. Now, he didn't want his daughter to ever think of her again—at least not by their hands.

Riley nodded, and didn't push him on it, though she looked curious. Dinner was a somber affair. He had the idea she knew she was about to get news she wasn't going to like.

Both of them made the effort to ensure Zoe didn't pick up on it. They were engaged and happy for her, but quiet otherwise.

Riley put Zoe to bed at eight, and when Oliver was alone, he took a deep breath and prepared himself for the conversation. Riley came back downstairs and sat next to him at the dining room table, hands folded in front of her.

She was putting on a good show, but he could see she was nervous.

"So," she said. "What's going on? You're not about to break up with me, right?" There was a small, weak smile after she said it. It was probably meant to be a joke, but Oliver doubted she was actually joking.

"What? No. I'm not breaking up with you."

Riley let out a long breath. "Thank God. You keep looking at me like you're about to break my heart."

"I'm never going to do that," he said. "I love you too much."

Riley nodded, her cheeks red. He hated she had thought he was about to end things with her, but he hated what he was about to say even more.

"I can't go into too much detail, but my company is getting sued by an employee."

"Oh my God. Like the company is going under kind of sued?"

"No," Oliver said. "Companies usually have savings for lawsuits. My dad and I were prepared for a billing lawsuit or something to do with the mess that is the healthcare system, but this is about an employee that didn't feel like they could take their breaks."

"I thought your company really tried to promote work-life balance. It was the main reason why Amanda wanted to work there."

"We do. Well, did. With the economy, our investors decided we needed to slim down our spending and ensure our operations were as cheap as possible. That's where Richard came in."

"The COO's name is Richard? That's the perfect name for him from what I've heard."

Oliver chuckled despite his mood. "He lives up to it, that's for sure. Anyway, he made some very strict policies. One my dad and I don't agree with, but our hands were tied because we're not publicly traded, and our investors help fund things when we don't have the cash on hand."

"Like I did with Camilla."

"Exactly," he said. "This is just on a bigger scale, and we have to keep them content unless we want to go public, which, honestly, after this, might be the better option."

"So, basically this Richard guy made some strict policies and is now getting sued for them."

"Right, and it's fallen on me as the CFO to provide a lot of documentation since the VP of HR quit a while ago. And it's too much for me to handle."

"Are you trying to tell me you have to hire an assistant or something? Is that the bad news?"

"We're not hiring an assistant," he said. "Richard found someone who was more than willing to do it. Someone who neither of us like."

Riley frowned, but then she put two and two together.

"It's not Sophie, is it?"

Oliver nodded.

"Fuck," she said. "There's no way you can choose someone else?"

"I don't know many people who will want to defend us against the employee who is probably justified in suing us. And Richard chose her, not me. I tried to get out of it, and my dad suggested that Richard could do the day-to-day communication, so I won't be working directly with her, but she's still got an in."

Riley shook her head, looking a mix between angry and . . . scared.

He waited. He waited for her to tell him not to see Sophie, or to find a way to get him off this project. She had a right to ask that of him considering her past and how she'd been betrayed. He wouldn't blame her if she screamed or cried about it. She had been through enough, and he hated that this was happening to add to it.

"You would tell me if you still had feelings for her, right?"

Of all the things he expected her to say, it wasn't that.

"Riley, I *never* want to look at her again. She hurt Zoe, and because of that, she hurt me."

"I know, but . . . you know how she looks."

"I'm not interested in how she looks. I couldn't have cared less the very moment she admitted she pushed Zoe."

Riley looked at him, seeing the truth in his eyes.

"I believe you," she said, sighing. "I really do, but this is . . . unnerving for me."

"I knew it would be, which is why I told you instead of hiding it. If I hid it then it would look worse."

"You were right to tell me. I don't think I could handle not knowing."

"And you have a right to be nervous, but you can trust me."

"I know," she said. "I don't want to be so nervous about everything, but I am, and I hate it."

"It's going to be okay. I don't feel anything for her, and if it makes you feel better, she only dug her hole deeper when she tried to talk to me today."

"Oh, this I have to know." Her lips formed a tiny smile.

"She accused Zoe of testing her mentally which was why she did what she did."

Riley laughed. "No way. That's a terrible excuse."

"I don't think she knows how to talk to people. She relies on her looks."

"Well, they *are* nice. But I'm glad you're seeing through it. Thank you for telling me." She smiled at him again, and this time, it was a gentle, open one. Oliver knew he had done the right thing. He walked over to her and planted a kiss on her lips.

"Thank you for being the most patient girlfriend ever."

"I doubt that. I did call someone an unloved fucker while driving to work."

Oliver laughed. "That's a new one."

"I must be a creative soul."

He laughed again, loving how things could feel so easy after such a hard conversation. He brushed her cheek with his thumb, relishing her smooth skin. She leaned into the touch, eyes fluttering closed.

"I love you," he reminded her. He felt it deep in his chest. This was a peace he'd never known until her.

"I love you too," she echoed. She was still smiling, but he could see the trepidation in her pursed lips. She looked at him like he was going to break her heart, and he couldn't wait until he proved that he never would.

Chapter Five

Riley

Riley woke up with the distant memory of an unpleasant dream. Her body buzzed with the feeling of a betrayal that slipped from her mind.

Oliver was next to her, still asleep, his arm slung over her waist. The weight in her chest didn't completely lift but seeing him helped lessen it.

As she tried to remember what she'd dreamt about, only two things came to mind: Oliver and Sophie.

There was something about what David did that changed her forever. Since they started dating, Oliver had done nothing of the sort to warrant these feelings, but she still looked for clues that weren't there.

Riley did believe he wouldn't go back to someone who had hurt Zoe. And while she didn't understand why he had chosen her, of all people, she did believe he had Zoe's best interests in mind. Sophie wasn't good for her.

But her mind raced regardless.

She let out a long breath as she remembered her first therapy appointment.

Despite not wanting to go, she climbed out of bed and dressed. As she sipped on her coffee, she wondered if this was even going to help.

She didn't realize her anxiety was growing until her gaze fell onto the now-empty liquor cabinet.

Rarely, a craving to solve her problems with alcohol popped up, but she refused to give into those; she had been keeping herself as distracted as possible to prevent an accidental slip.

And now with the added stress of Sophie being back in Oliver's life, she was feeling that desire to drink again.

It was settled. She needed to give therapy a shot.

The therapist was a woman in her mid-thirties named Sally. Riley had read her profile before making an appointment, and this person specialized in drinking problems in women. Sally promised a warm and welcoming environment free from judgment. Riley wasn't so sure such a place existed.

She was, after all, very used to being judged for her choices.

Her hands shook as she drove to the appointment. It didn't help that this place was in a part of town she hated driving to.

Luckily, getting there wasn't too bad. The waiting room was nice, and before Riley could get bored, Sally came out to introduce herself and lead Riley to her office.

Sally's office was in the back corner of a large building and held one couch and a chair. There was a tissue box looming on the small table next to the patient's seat. Riley wondered how long it would be until she reached for them.

"What brings you in today, Riley?"

What a loaded first question.

"Um, well, I have problems. Not huge problems, but problems nonetheless. They're so small that I'm not even sure that I should be here."

"Okay," Sally said, smiling. "If you feel comfortable, tell me about these problems."

"They're all a part of my past. These days, things are actually pretty great. I'm in a healthy relationship. I have stable housing, and a better connection with my mom. But . . . a year ago, things were very different."

"What was your life like a year ago?"

"My long-term boyfriend cheated on me. I had a drinking problem. And my mom regularly praised my sister and berated me."

"That is a lot to go through."

"There's more. My ex cheated on me with my best friend, who was my only friend. So, my support system was completely gone. I had to rebuild my life."

"Who is in your support system now?"

"My new boyfriend, who also used to be my boss. I made a new friend, and she also used to be my boss, but she's not really anymore; we're business partners now. There's also the little girl I adopted. She's the daughter of my boyfriend. She's obviously not supporting me necessarily, but she makes me want to be better."

"You adopted a child too?"

Riley carefully regarded Sally, as she did anyone who heard that she had adopted Zoe. She gave the slightest of nods to confirm.

"Congratulations," Sally said. "That's a huge accomplishment."

"Thanks," she said, relief making her shoulders lower. "She didn't have a mother in her life, and now she does."

"What's your relationship like with her father, then? He was your boss. Now he is your boyfriend?"

Riley waited for the judgment again, maybe a curve of the brow or a tightness in the lips. It never came.

"It's good. He's kind and patient. He cares about both me and his daughter. It took some trial and error for us to get together, but we do truly love each other."

"So, when did this adoption happen?"

"Before we were together, actually. Oliver was always more concerned with Zoe's happiness, and he told me there was no one he'd rather share her with. We started dating officially after that."

Sally nodded as she jotted down a note in her spiralbound.

Riley eyed the movement. Was there something wrong with what she said?

"I'm writing down details you tell me so I can remember them better. I do this for all of my clients," Sally explained. "I'm not writing down anything judgmental."

"I was that obvious, huh?"

"No, but I've worked with many people. They all feel like me writing is a sign. I assure you—I am not here to judge. I am here to help."

"Sometimes I find those two coincide."

"Does that happen with anyone in particular?"

"It used to with my mother. A lot, actually. She really favored my sister, and she even admitted she did it because I look like my dad who left when I was kid. With my sister, she would take a gentle approach, but with me . . . well, she wasn't as gentle. But we've talked about it, and she knows she was wrong."

Sally nodded. "That sounds difficult."

"It could have been worse. She could have left like my dad did."

"I suppose that's true, but she was still your mother. Parental love should be unconditional, and it sounds like hers was not. Favoritism is painful."

Riley knew for a fact it was. She took a deep breath, knowing she wanted to shrug it off rather than admit it.

"You're right, but she apologized for it, and I'm fine now. I have a good job and a good boyfriend. I have no reason to feel the way I do."

"And how do you feel?"

"Like . . . everything is going to fall apart." Riley's eyes darted to her hands, shame heating her cheeks. "It's so stupid."

"I don't think it is. Yes, you've worked through a lot of things on your own. You've adopted a little girl and rebuilt your support system. I'm sure there's more because you seem like a strong and capable woman."

"I'm really not."

Sally smiled. "Why do you think that?"

"Because I did all of this so late. I partied and drank for so long before I finally came to my senses. The drinking caused half of my problems."

"And you stopped?"

"Yes, when I met Zoe. And I've stuck to it, even when I feel pain."

"What is hurting you?"

"Sometimes it's my sister. Other times . . . I'm not sure. No one else is hurting me, so I want it to stop."

"Why do you need to stop it?"

"It's pain. It's not good to feel pain."

"Our emotions need to be felt, even pain."

"But if I let myself feel it, then it's never going away."

"You'd be surprised at how our emotions change when we give them time. When we allow ourselves to work through the emotions instead of bottling them up, it's much easier, and healthier, to process them and move forward."

Riley wasn't so sure, but she eyed the degree on the wall. This woman was properly trained, and Camilla had said it worked.

"Then what do I need to do?"

"I think we should see each other weekly. I can learn about you and provide guidance on how to move forward. If we need to go up or down from there, we can decide then."

Riley sighed. Going weekly meant she needed to tell Oliver, and she had no idea how he would react. If this were David, he would laugh at her. Sarah would too.

But Oliver wasn't either of them. He'd been a better boyfriend than she'd ever imagined, and she didn't want to paint him with the same brush as David.

"Okay," she said. "I can make that work."

Sally gathered more information about her past, and then they worked out when Riley could come to therapy. When it was over, she felt exhausted, but a little hopeful. Maybe this would be good. Maybe she could stop feeling like everything was going to fall apart.

Oliver

"If this is bad news, it will need to wait until next week."

Oliver rarely called Jane—not because they didn't talk, but because he didn't have the time. When Jane answered the phone with her trademark deadpan, haughty tone, he wondered if she was in a bad mood, or if maybe it was a good idea to call at all.

"It's not," Oliver said. "I'm on my way home from work. I wanted to run an idea by you."

"Oh?"

He fought against the anxiety in his chest. "I was thinking about asking Riley to marry me."

"*My* Riley?"

"Yes," he said. "Why do you seem surprised?"

If there was one thing Oliver grew tired of, it was people questioning why he was with Riley. It oddly only happened with people who *knew* Riley, as if they thought her personality was the reason why they weren't a good match. Sure, Oliver was more closed off with people he didn't know, but he had never been like that with her.

"I'm not sure," Jane said, frowning. "I worry about her slipping, and then pushing you away."

"I wouldn't leave if she slipped," Oliver said.

"She mentioned Zoe's mother had problems with drinking."

"Riley *is* Zoe's mother."

"Sorry, birth mother."

Oliver pushed down his annoyance and continued on. "Zoe's birth mother did have a drinking problem, but if she wanted to stick around, I would have worked with her. But she and I were different in what we wanted and we never talked about things like that. Riley and I do. I know she wants to be better, and that's a lot more than could ever be said about Zoe's birth mother."

Jane nodded. "Then I suppose I have no reason to be surprised."

"So, what do you think about it?"

"I think it's great. You already share a daughter and a home. Have you spoken with her about marriage?"

"Not yet. I was hoping for it to be a surprise."

"Oh, I don't know. Riley does poorly with surprises."

Oliver frowned. He always saw himself being the one to pick the ring and arrange a grand proposal. That was how his dad did it with his mom, and he wasn't sure he was ready to change his plans.

"So, I should maybe talk to her first?"

"I'm not sure," Jane said, sounding more confused than he'd ever heard her. "I'll be honest, I never expected her to marry."

"Because of the drinking?"

"Because of David. He was never the marrying type—at least not when he was with Riley. I assumed she would always stay with him and I gave up any hope of seeing her get married. I doubted she ever would. I can tell you that she was not a fan of Amanda's wedding. She's never been the traditional type."

Yes, Oliver definitely knew that was true. Maybe that was his hang-up. He couldn't see her doing things the usual way—the way he saw things playing out in his mind.

"What made you decide on marriage?" Jane asked.

"I've always wanted it. I really settled on it with Riley when Zoe's teacher accidentally called her my wife. I know we've only been together for a few months, but I've known her a lot longer, and I feel like she's the one."

"I think you two are a great match," Jane said. "But I do worry that David did more damage that she would like to admit."

"I know." Oliver's voice was hard. "I've seen it."

"I do not think it's a bad idea to ask her, but I truly don't know how Riley is doing these days. I don't think she ever dealt with David leaving her, and I wonder if she ever will. That would be the only issue I can think of."

"I can probably ask how she's doing without giving myself away. We tend to avoid the conversation of exes. Both of us have some bad ones that we don't like mentioning."

"It's sometimes necessary to talk about it. Look at me, I avoided my own ex and damaged my relationship with my daughter."

She was right. If he avoided asking how Riley was doing, then they would never actually talk about it.

"I'm going to talk to her," he said firmly.

"Let me know how it goes. You should come by some time if you do plan on going through with this. I have my mother's ring. Riley always wanted it."

"That sounds perfect," Oliver said. "I will come by to get it. Thank you," he added genuinely. "This means a lot to me."

"It means a lot to me too," she said, and he could hear the smile in her voice. "I hope Riley says yes. She would be a fool not to."

When Oliver hung up with Jane, he was almost home from work. It was later than he liked, but he could see the living room light was on, which meant Riley was still awake.

When he walked in, she sat up quickly, turning to him while biting her lip.

Oliver's plan for the night quickly went up in smoke. "What's wrong?"

"How did you know something was wrong?" she asked.

"Because I know you," he replied. "What's going on?"

She opened her mouth to answer, but then closed it. She struggled for a long moment before she put her head in her hands.

He grew increasingly worried.

"Riley," he said, coming to kneel in front of her. "You can tell me anything."

That seemed to help. She lifted her face out her hands, and he could see her cheeks were pink. "I . . . I don't want you to think I'm weak or that there's something wrong with me."

"You can tell me anything," he repeated as he grabbed her hand. "It can be that you started drinking again, or that you're thinking of dyeing your hair green. I won't think any less of you."

"I . . . I did want to drink, but instead of doing that I . . . went to therapy."

Oliver waited for the next part of it.

She only stared back. "You're not going to say anything?"

"I'm still waiting for you to tell me what you're upset about."

"I'm in therapy," she repeated. "I don't feel like myself, so I decided to go talk to a stranger about it."

"Riley, therapy isn't a bad thing. I had to get it when Zoe was two because of how hard her first year was on me. I even considered going back after what happened with Sophie."

"You did?"

"As a parent, you have to get used to the idea of it if you want to be better for your kids. I know a lot of moms go through postpartum depression after giving birth. I think I went through the single dad version of that—if that even exists. And then went through it again right before you moved in here. Riley, therapy is a great tool to use to get better. You thought I would judge you for it?"

She bit her lip. "I hoped you wouldn't, but in my house, therapy was for people who had real problems, and if you went, you were either being dramatic or were weak."

"That explains a lot about your family."

"I didn't know how you would react."

"I'd never think anything negative. After what David and Sarah put you through, I wouldn't be surprised to hear you need it, and that doesn't include all the things Amanda and your mom have done over the years. It's okay. I'm not judging you."

Riley's shoulders sagged. She let out a long breath. "Thank God. I haven't even worked out *my* feelings on therapy, but I was so worried it was a mistake and that I'd be criticized for it."

"Admitting you need help is hard. Getting help for things you are struggling with is one of the toughest things you can do," he said. "And after everything you've been through, I understand why you would want to talk to a professional. If there's anything I can do, you know I'll do it."

Riley shook her head. "I'll be okay. Thank you for offering."

He nodded, but his chest burned with the desire to fix this. Oliver racked his brain for something he could buy that would make all of this go away. When nothing came up, he grew frustrated. Maybe money couldn't solve the problem, but what else could he offer?

Her arms wrapped around him, bringing him out of his thoughts. She hugged him tightly, like she was stranded in an ocean and he was the only thing keeping her afloat.

Oliver made sure to hug her back just as tightly.

He would have never let her go, but she yawned loudly.

"Time for bed?" he asked.

"I don't even have the energy to get up," she muttered.

"That's an easy problem to solve."

She looked at him questioningly, but he stood and hoisted her up.

Riley yelped, arms wrapping around his neck. "Wh-what are you doing? I'm way too heavy to—"

"It's fine," he said. "It's much easier to carry you to our room than it is to get Zoe up all the stairs."

"I can—"

"Let me do this for you," he said firmly. "Please."

Her cheeks turned pink, but she didn't protest.

Huh. Maybe he'd found the magic words to get her to listen to him.

Oliver carried her to bed, gently putting her on her preferred side of the mattress. Her cheeks were still pink, and he pressed a kiss to the warm skin before he stood up straight.

"Th-thank you. I'm so—" He put a finger to her lips.

"No," Oliver said. "No apologies. I wanted to do that."

She kept her mouth shut. He was almost shocked she listened, but once he realized he'd finally gotten her to let him do something they both wanted, his chest warmed in satisfaction.

Oh, he was *definitely* remembering this for later. Especially if it was a way for him to treat Riley like he always wanted to.

Chapter Six

Riley

It was Riley's birthday.

The heat of summer still stuck around, despite pumpkin spice lattes being in style at the shop, and everyone decorating like the leaves were turning orange, even though they wouldn't until late October.

Riley wasn't sure her birthday deserved much fanfare. She was turning twenty-seven, which was a rather boring age. This was, however, the first birthday she was spending with Oliver, as his girlfriend no less, and she knew he loved to celebrate Zoe's.

But a five-year-old's birthday was different than a twenty-seven-year old's. While she hoped he at least acknowledged the day, she didn't know what she wanted beyond that.

After two therapy sessions, Riley was slowly learning she had come to expect what David had always given her, and David wasn't much of a giver.

Her last five birthdays she had bought herself flowers and a cake. David would wish her a happy birthday, but would immediately return to his video games without giving her a second thought. He never celebrated much of anything for *her.*

For his birthdays, however, he always wanted the day to himself. He didn't want to do chores—not that he did them any other day—and only wanted to play games with his online friends, and then have Riley take him out to eat.

Over time, Riley's birthday had soured, because she knew deep down that David wasn't playing fair. He always wanted special treatment on his big day, but hers felt like nothing more than an inconvenience.

David had treated her only slightly better than her father did. He acknowledged when she came home, when she left, and nothing else.

That wasn't what Riley had wanted in a relationship. When she was young, she would dream of someone who would shower her with attention and love.

When she met David, she thought that was a child's dream, and that every partner grew distant when they got comfortable with one another.

She wasn't sure what to think about her current relationship with Oliver.

Because she didn't want to be away from him. At work, when she had a second to breathe, she would think about him and wonder how his day was going. She would imagine the way his lips felt on hers and how he held her when they slept.

It was alarming just how much space Zoe and Oliver took up in her mind.

Sally had told her it was perfectly healthy to feel this way, as long as Riley didn't lose herself in the process.

The problem was, she would be one hundred percent willing to lose herself if it meant making Oliver happy.

And that, Sally had told her, was how David had taken advantage of her.

But the main difference between Oliver and David was their expectations. Riley couldn't imagine Oliver asking her to change because he never had. She'd come into his life without ever thinking they would date, so she had always been able to be herself. He had told her he loved her while she wore flannels, never had her hair down, and worked in a coffee shop. He'd never once asked her to dress a different way, change her personality, or do anything she didn't want.

And while there were no signs the end was near, she felt like it was.

Riley had been given deep breathing exercises for now. They helped, but they didn't stop the feeling that everything would end. Camilla had warned her after the first session that therapy took time, because you couldn't get through everything in one forty-five-minute appointment, so she was working on being patient.

Oliver had been more than understanding. He asked how they went, and if she was comfortable talking about it. He'd ordered food for them even on the days she didn't have therapy, saying she needed to relax rather than cook.

It was . . . odd, to say the least. Riley thought the news of her therapy wouldn't change much, but he was making an effort. More than that, even.

The morning of her birthday, she laid in bed waiting for either Zoe or Oliver to come and wake her. She was exhausted after working an eight-hour shift before having to pick Zoe up from school; and of course, on her way out of the classroom, she had run into the snobby mom.

Luckily, the other mom didn't say anything, but she gave Riley a look that told her she didn't belong. She was stuck between wanting to flip her off and crawling into a hole to hide.

It hadn't been fun.

Thankfully, Riley got a whole thirty minutes in before Zoe burst through the door.

"Happy birthday, Mommy!"

Riley smiled, despite her tiredness. Zoe never failed to put her in a good mood. "Thank you, kiddo."

"I held her back as long as I could," Oliver said. He was carrying a tray. "Here's breakfast."

"In bed?"

"It's the best place to have it."

She blushed. She'd never had breakfast in bed. One time she tried while hungover, and David had complained for weeks about crumbs.

This was what she wanted, but it felt so undeserved.

"Thank you," she replied, smiling through her discomfort. "Did you make this?"

"Unfortunately, no," Oliver said. "I woke up a little too late to put this together. I ordered it from Pancake Pantry."

"Oh, I've never had it before." Mostly because anything in the vicinity of Oliver's neighborhood was expensive. "Is it good?"

He laughed. "It's famous actually, but I think that's more because it's been around forever and it also happens to be Taylor Swift's favorite place."

"Wait, what?"

"It's always amusing to see how little you know about the music scene here, and you even worked at a downtown bar."

"I tuned out the music," she said. "There are two types of Nashville locals—the ones who like country music, and the ones who are like me who totally ignore that side of the city."

"I must land somewhere in the middle, but my dad likes country music. I never saw much of the appeal."

"At least Nashville's food is good."

She glanced down at the plate of food. Fresh eggs, with pancakes and bacon.

Oliver sat on the bed next to her. "They also have fresh orange juice. Try it."

Riley took a sip, and it *was* amazing. It tasted nothing like what she could buy at the store. Zoe hopped on the bed on the other side of her, asking for bites of the food too. Oliver tried to stop her, but she has happy to share.

After breakfast, Oliver pulled her out of bed. Apparently, he had plans. She fought the desire to tell him she didn't need all of this, that her birthday wasn't special.

But she *did* want this. A part of her felt so grateful to him that she didn't know if she could handle it. The better a man Oliver was, the more scared she was that she didn't measure up.

He took her to the Opryland Resort, which housed a huge plant conservatory with lovely scenery. Riley had been a few times when she was a kid. She and Amanda would walk through the beautiful areas with wide eyes. When Jane could afford it, they'd also stop to get ice cream while they looked at all the plants. To this day, Amanda's house was filled with houseplants in honor of their small tradition. It was possibly one of the more touristy things she used to do as a child. But Jane never had the expendable money, and the gardens were free if you knew where to park.

Riley wasn't sure how Oliver knew, but she was grateful to get to see it all again.

When he revealed they had reservations at a restaurant in one of the conservatories, she balked at how expensive it must have been.

But he led her to a table overlooking the fountains with a patient and calm smile. The fountains used to be her favorite place when she was little.

It was perfection.

While they ate, Riley intently watched the water show, laughing at the kids who walked around the wet ground hoping to be sprayed. Eventually, Zoe begged to join in, so Oliver paid for their meals and let her play with some of the other kids.

After she tired out, they walked around to some of the hidden corners Riley used to love exploring.

The hotel was a gorgeous place, and people often got married underneath the enchanting scenery. This day was no different. There was a small wedding party in one of the many alcoves of the building. Riley's eyes were drawn to the bride in the distance. She looked radiant.

"What are you looking at?" Oliver asked softly.

"The wedding over there." She pointed. "It's such a perfect place to get married, but so expensive. I looked it up once a long time ago."

Back when she thought there was a chance she and David were going to get married.

"It can't be that bad," he replied. "Would you want to get married here?"

"Me? Married?" Riley shook her head. "I don't know. I haven't thought about that in a long time."

He frowned. "Why not?"

She hadn't realized what he was hinting at for a moment, but when she did, her face grew warm.

"Well, David didn't want to get married. At least not to me. And we've only dated for a few months," she added, gesturing between the two of them. "I didn't think you'd be worried about it."

"I was thinking about marrying Sophie within weeks."

"Yeah, but you weren't thinking clearly because you were doing it all with Zoe. There's no rush or anything. It's not like I'm going anywhere."

Unless you want me to.

The thought came unbidden, and she fought against a wave of anxiety. This wasn't what she wanted to be thinking about, not on such a nice day.

"Do *you* think there's no rush?" he asked.

"I . . . I don't know what I think," she admitted. "Marriage is something I always wanted, but after so long of being kept at arm's length, I think I started to believe it wasn't something I could ever have. Or that it was okay that I wasn't going to have it. That's not *your* fault, though, Oliver. Maybe I need to bring it up to Sally . . ."

"Whatever you need to do," he said softly, giving Riley a small smile.

She looked up at him gratefully. She didn't know what she did to deserve such a patient man.

"I love you," she said, sliding her arms around his middle. His hands came to wrap around hers.

"I love you too," he said. "And for the record, I'm not going anywhere, either."

She was still working to believe that, but his words lifted just a bit of weight off her chest.

"This was a perfect day," she said.

"It's not over yet." He checked his phone. "I think we can go back to the house now."

"What did you do?" Fear crept into her chest, but her body buzzed with a bit of excitement to see whatever this surprise was.

"Just something you wanted."

She glared at him doubtfully. When they pulled into the driveway, nothing looked amiss, but then she spotted her car.

"Did you . . . get my windows tinted?"

"Good catch," he said. "I had them do your windshield too. It's all street legal, but it should help your eyes."

"I . . . I don't know what to say."

"You should say thank you!" Zoe called.

"Thank you," she replied, her face warm.

"It was no problem. I couldn't *not* get you anything for your birthday."

As much as Riley hated to admit it, she was thankful she didn't have to fork over the money herself. While it wouldn't have broken the bank, she wanted to save the money for Zoe.

"That's not all," he informed her. "I may have made a slight system upgrade."

"What?" Riley asked.

"Did you know your model year is the only one eligible to have the infotainment system upgraded?"

"What in the world is *infotainment?*"

"The system your car uses for music and audio controls."

"Oh. Wait, was it expensive?"

"Nope," he said. "You should turn on your car and see what it does."

With her heart in her throat, Riley did. There was a phone cord she didn't remember having. She slowly plugged it in and was shocked to see her phone's screen displayed on the screen.

"Holy shit."

She could see her texts and a map displaying the streets around her. It was incredible in comparison to the simple display she was used to.

"Oliver, this is . . ." *Expensive. Undeserved. Desired.* "Awesome."

"It's your birthday," he said. "I had to get something for you."

"I still feel like I should pay you back."

"You don't pay back gifts. Just enjoy it, Riley. That's how you can pay me back."

She eyed him warily, just like the night when he'd picked her up and carried her to bed. Where was the eye roll or the not-so-hidden annoyance at doing something for her?

But it simply wasn't there. All she saw was Oliver looking at her with an easy smile.

"Thank you," she said. "This is amazing."

And it was. She couldn't deny that.

"Can we go get ice cream in Mommy's car?" Zoe asked.

"If she wants to," Oliver said.

Ice cream sounded like the perfect conclusion to the day. "Let's do it."

Oliver

It had been weeks since Oliver made his usual trip to Riley's coffee shop.

It was late, but he thought she should be working. She usually did on Tuesday nights since the shop extended their hours to allow for more events in the evening.

It was only when he walked in that he remembered that she'd purposefully traded this shift with Camilla in order to watch Zoe.

He came in right at close, as all the customers were leaving. Camilla was wiping a table in the back of the shop and looked up when he walked in.

"Oliver?" she asked, frowning. "What are you doing here? Is everything okay with Riley?"

"I totally blanked on Riley's schedule. I thought she'd be here."

"You're working too much."

"I am. I should go before I make more of a fool of myself."

"You don't have to. I could use company while closing. We never get to talk, and I'd like to know the man my best friend is in love with."

"Then I'll stay for a few."

"How are things?"

"Things are good," he said. "I'm thinking about proposing to Riley but—"

Camilla interrupted him. "That's huge! Congratulations."

"I actually don't know when it will happen. Riley's been . . . off lately."

"Honestly, it's not surprising considering what she's been through."

"I agree. Her mom said a surprise was a bad idea, and I want this to be right, but I'm not even sure this is the *right* time."

Camilla's lips twisted into another frown. "Maybe it's not. She's really going through something. I get the vibe she thinks you're going to leave."

"Obviously not," he said.

"So proposing would prove her wrong, but then again, she could freak out and try to convince you out of it."

"What do you think I should do?" he asked. "You know her just as well as I do."

Camilla blinked. "I don't know. I know she's in therapy. Maybe it's going to help. Maybe she just needs a little time."

"I don't want to do this and make things worse, but I can't stop thinking about how I want her to be my wife. So how do *I* make her feel better?"

Camilla smiled sadly. "You don't."

"What? How can that be the solution?"

"Because it's her pain to deal with."

"But I should be able to do something."

"Things don't exactly work out the way we want them to. You're there for her every day. You're proving her fears wrong. That's all you can do. And besides, this is Riley we're talking about. She's so smart. You know she'll come out of this stronger."

"I know." He nodded. "And I agree I should probably wait, but it's so hard. I know Riley is going through a lot because of her ex. I won't lie, if I saw him, I'd consider taking a few swings at him."

"You and me both," Camilla muttered. "You're way better than what I've heard about him."

Oliver knew that, and he hated him for it. "I do wish I could do *more*."

"Let her fix it. I know it's hard. I want nothing more than for my best friend to feel like she can ask anything she wants from me, but if we try to fix it, then we're taking her power away from her."

"How do you know for sure? The last thing I want to do is make her feel like I'm not doing everything I can."

"I know because I've been through this," Camilla explained. "I'm a lesbian and my parents are homophobic. When I was caught kissing my now wife, they kicked me out. She tried everything in her power to make sure I was okay, and I let her for a long time, but the pain was still mine and it made things worse for me. And then I decided I had to deal with it myself. No one else could do it for me."

Oliver blinked at the weight of her admission. "Camilla, I'm sorry I brought it—"

"No," she interrupted. "It's okay. I don't mind sharing it with you. I felt like an example would help you understand. I know it's going to be hard to step back and let her do her thing, but being supported is all she needs."

"And what if it's not enough?"

"I have a feeling you'll find a way to do enough. If she came to you tomorrow and asked you to treat her in a different way, would you?"

"If it helped her, yes."

"Then you're on the right track. Give her time, and when you're ready, ask her."

Oliver nodded, but it was a bitter pill to swallow.

"Out of curiosity, though," Camilla continued, "what ring are you getting her? I can't see her wearing any jewelry."

"Jane agreed to give me a family ring. She said Riley has always wanted it."

"Oh, I can't wait to see her face when you propose."

"I'll be sure you're there," he said, smiling. He checked his watch. "I should probably get home. I have a future wife to see."

"And I have a present wife to see. It was good talking to you, Oliver."

He said his goodbyes and headed home. He was more than ready to see Riley after a long day.

He pulled into the driveway and let out a deep breath. He was thankful he talked to Camilla; it helped him repress the urge to try to fix everything for Riley when it's what she may not want or need from him right now.

Riley was walking down the stairs as he entered the house. It was past Zoe's bedtime, and he hated being so late, but he was happy to know she was here for her.

"You had a late night," Riley said. Her voice was off. Uncertainty.

"Uh, yeah. That project is killing us all. I made Richard stay late to assign work to Sophie. And then I dropped by the coffee shop."

"Why?"

"Well, I thought you were there, but it was Camilla. Then I stayed to chat with her."

"What did you talk about?"

"Um, life?"

He was a terrible liar.

She narrowed her eyes at him. Her arms, crossed over her chest, were tight with tension. "Life?" Her voice was low.

"It wasn't anything bad," he said, unnerved by her tone. "Wait, was it a problem I stopped to talk to Camilla?"

"Yes," she began harshly. Then she shook her head. "No." A pause. "I'm not sure."

"What's wrong?"

"Nothing. I mean nothing *should* be." Riley took a deep breath, and finally met his gaze. "The last time my boyfriend had a conversation alone with my best friend, it didn't end well for me."

Realization hit him.

"Riley," he rushed to say. "I never—"

"No, I know. It's so stupid to think like that. Camilla is married, and isn't even interested in men. There's no way that would happen again."

"If I knew it was going to upset you, I would have never gone."

"Don't apologize. I don't want to be one of those controlling girlfriends who say their boyfriends can't talk to other women. I *don't*, but . . ."

"You're still stuck in the past."

Riley sighed, and then nodded. "I'm sorry," she said sadly. "I don't want to compare you to David. I know it's gotta be insulting."

"I'm more worried about you," he replied. "I know you don't truly believe anything is going on, but I didn't mean to take you back to what happened last year."

"I know." She sounded frustrated. He didn't know if it was at him or herself. "You would never do that. This is a totally different situation, but it's like the moment I think about you being with Camilla, it's like it's happening all over again."

Her voice broke, and she closed her eyes, fighting back tears.

"I fucking hate that they did this to me."

Oliver wanted to sweep her away and make her never feel this again. He would move the entire earth if it meant she would be okay. No amount of money or time could stop him from wishing she had never met David.

But he couldn't take this from her.

"Do you want to talk about it?" he asked instead.

"Come on, you're my boyfriend. I'm sure you don't want to hear about an ex more than you already have."

"I don't want to hear about you being in pain, no. But if talking would help, then I'm here. I've always been your friend, even before we dated."

"Okay," she said, sighing. "But I want a hot chocolate for this."

He felt his chest loosen, and he went to make her what she wanted without complaint. Once the warm drink was in her hand, they sat on the couch.

"You know how it ended," she said. "You know I walked in on them talking about how they would break it to me and how I stormed out of there. But what I don't talk about is . . . what it was like before I caught them. After some time, I looked back and realized how much they were keeping from me—how obvious it was."

"How long were Sarah and David together?"

"I never got a clear answer, but they started acting weird months before I found out. Sarah was distant. David didn't ever look me in the eye. We stopped having sex and even touching. Sarah ignored my texts and calls. I thought it was because she had just lost her job and David had just gotten a new game but . . ." She trailed off for a long moment. "I guess it was because they were seeing each other behind my back."

Oliver had never hated people that he'd never met more than Sarah and David. While he knew what they did was bad, hearing the details made it worse. To not only betray Riley in such a way, but then to ignore her?

It was terrible.

"I still wonder why sometimes," she continued. "Not that I ever want to be with David again, but could I have done something differently? Could I *be* different to make sure this never happens again?"

"Riley, the problem was with them, not you."

"But then that meant I couldn't stop it, and that I can't stop it in the future either, and that's so much worse. I love my life. I love you and Zoe. If I can't be better in order to prevent me from ever feeling this again, then what can I do?"

"You can trust that I'm not going anywhere," he said. "Ever since I fell for you, I've never looked at another woman. I don't care about anyone else, because you're it for me."

"But what if I get busy and we drift apart?"

"We're busy now and we're not drifting apart, right?"

She looked at her hands.

"Right?" he asked again. "We still talk. We sleep in the same bed. I know we don't have sex *every* night but I thought it was mutual thing—"

"It's not that," she said, face red. "We have a child and both of us have been tired. That's the thing about what I'm feeling, it's not logical. We *are* close. We make time for each other despite our overloaded schedules but . . . it's still new. Will we do this in five years? Will my personality get old and boring?"

"No," he said without hesitation.

"How can you *know* that?"

"Because in five years, you won't be the same person. Neither will I. But when we made a commitment to each other, that included growing *together*. Not apart. Maybe we'll fall off the track, but if you love someone, you don't give up on them because of something simple. You fight for it, and I will do that. Will you?"

"Of course," she said.

"You're used to having a man letting you do all the bending and breaking in a relationship. That's not me, Riley. I hope I've proven that to you. If not between us, then with Zoe."

"No, you have," she said. "I guess I never thought of it that way. I've been so worried that I'll mess up something or that you'll find someone else."

"I'm with you forever, Riley. I mean it."

"You can't promise that."

"You're right. Forever isn't promised, but I do know I'll be with you as long as I can."

"I guess I just don't get why. I mean, it's *me*."

"And that's enough," he said. "Has this come up with your therapist?"

"She tells me I need to work on my self-esteem."

"I can see that."

"I . . . I'm sorry," she eventually said. "I'm sorry I'm struggling with this. I have no reason to. Not with you."

"If you ever need anything from me, or need me to do anything differently with you, let me know."

"I don't want to change who you are."

"Think about it not as change, but as growth."

She smiled. "That's a good way to look at it."

His chest loosened at the brightness of her grin. It wasn't much, but he loved that he made her feel better.

He wished he could do more. He wished he could take her heart and heal it—take away all the pain of her past.

But he couldn't. Instead, he held onto her like she was everything to him because she was, and he'd spend every day proving that to her.

Chapter Seven

Riley

Riley was back in therapy. She sat against the gray couch and stared at the ominous tissue box in front of her.

Sally had just heard the details about Oliver seeing Camilla. It had been hard to talk about with him the night before, but it was much harder to open up to someone she'd only known a few weeks.

"That sounds very difficult for you to hear about."

"It shouldn't be," Riley replied. "Oliver wasn't doing anything suspicious. He also didn't lie to me about why he was late coming home."

"Of course not. But we all have experiences that shape our feelings, and from our last couple sessions, you've said you're worried he will leave you. Those things combined may have caused you to have an emotional reaction. You're fearful, and you've been betrayed by friends before."

"I know that, and so does he. He wasn't mad about it or anything. But I am."

"At him?"

"At myself. And at David and Sarah. I don't want to feel like this. I thought the happily ever after was supposed to be *happy*."

"It will be because you're here working on it. And I know what I want us to work on."

"What's that?"

"We haven't talked a lot about David. What went wrong with your relationship with him?"

Riley blinked. "Well, he cheated on me."

"Before that. Him cheating on you was his fault. It was wrong, but you've gotten so lost in the action that I don't believe you've talked about the relationship."

"I've done it a little. With Oliver."

"Then you've thought about it. That's good."

"Is this supposed to help? I've moved on."

"You know you're still feeling the pain of what happened in the past. I can understand being resistant to talking about this because you want to move forward, but in order to move forward, we have to accept what happened before. I know you must be scared—"

"I'm not," she insisted. "I've moved on. This is behind me."

Sally tilted her head, eyes narrowed. A question without words.

"I-I mean I should be. I want to be."

"Then let's give this a try."

Riley sighed. "Fine. What do you want to talk about?"

"What was your relationship with David like? What problems did you see?"

"He was selfish, and then he cheated on me."

"It sounds like he was, but I want to talk about *your* role in the relationship."

"I mean, I was a good girlfriend. I paid more than half the bills, I cleaned everything. It wasn't like it is with Oliver now, that's for sure."

"What was your connection like? Was there ever a time when things fizzled out?"

Riley blinked. "I don't know, but I don't think it matters."

"Riley," Sally said, voice stern. "You did *not* deserve to be cheated on. The problem will *always* lie with the person who stepped out of the relationship, but it is still important to look at where things went wrong, so you can freely admit when they're happening again."

"They're *not* happening again. I *love* Oliver."

"I agree, but I'm not talking about love. I'm talking about thinking about what you wanted in a relationship, the *connection* you desire, and seeing if you have it."

"I do."

"I think you need to prove that to *yourself*, not me. You have this fear that it will end, after all. So, let's look at the past and see what it changes now."

Riley sighed, leaning back in the chair. Sally had her there. "Okay. Fine. We'll try it."

Sally nodded, looking pleased.

She thought back to David. What he looked like, how he treated her when they met. It was pleasant.

"Well, to start, I don't . . . I don't think I even liked David—as a person, I mean. He was selfish, and bragged about everything he did."

"Why did you date him then?"

"Because on the rare times he did give me attention, it made me feel like I wasn't just Amanda's shadow. This was at a time she was beating me at *everything*. My mother always talked about how amazing she was doing."

"That sounds painful."

"It was, and when he would shut up about himself for ten minutes and talk about me, I felt special."

"But his lack of attention felt familiar."

Riley looked at her hands. "I think you're right."

"What happened over time?"

"I began working more to be out of the apartment. His selfishness only grew, and over time, he never seemed to look at me. But Amanda was married. So I thought I needed a stable relationship too."

"The favoritism and competition between you and Amanda took a toll," she said. "And while I'm grateful for your mother seeing her error on that, it's doesn't wipe away the pain. That damaged your self-esteem, Riley."

"I know," she said, her voice soft. "I basically have *no* self-esteem, especially in this relationship with Oliver that I care so much about. Every time he does something without me, I'm worried he's going to find someone else."

"I want you to try something. It's very easy and doesn't take much time."

"Okay," Riley said. "What is it?"

"It's a little cheesy, but I want you to look in the mirror each morning. Take yourself in and find *one* think you like. It may not seem like much, but it will help you gain some respect for yourself. That all starts within."

"I don't even know if I can find *one* thing I like," she muttered. "I mean, look at me. My hair is straight and lifeless, if you saw Amanda then you'd—" Riley cut herself off when Sally raised her eyebrows. "I just totally did what my mom used to do, didn't I?"

"Yes," Sally said. "Very good catch."

Riley groaned. "It doesn't help that Amanda is *still* causing me grief. Just a few weeks ago, she said that if the timing worked out right, it might have been her getting with Oliver and not me."

"Your sister said she wished she had ended up with *your* boyfriend?" Sally asked. When Riley nodded, her therapist shook her head. "That wasn't an appropriate comment, *and* it's irrelevant. He loves *you*."

"Sometimes I wonder if it was all timing, though. That he fell for me because I happened to be there when he was loneliest, not because I'm me. I highly doubt he likes my flannels, or my weird sense of humor, or how I basically took over his house with my things when I moved in."

"Flannels are popular for a reason," Sally said, smiling. "A lot of people love them."

"But they're not fashionable."

"Tell that to Target," she said, laughing.

Okay, maybe Sally had a point.

"There's nothing wrong with you for being yourself, but sometimes we forget. Tell me, when you feel this way, how do you typically handle that?"

"Usually, Zoe finds me, or I go to work."

"So you keep yourself busy."

"Yes. I don't want to feel bad."

"You mentioned you used to drink, yes?" she asked, and Riley's shame burned her cheeks. "I'm not saying it as a bad thing. There's no judgment, remember? But there is possibly an explanation for why you used to do it. Drinking can be an easy solution to problems because it lowers our inhibitions. For a short time, you can't feel."

"Well, yeah, but it ruined my life."

"Yes, because so many people in your life were against it, and because you now have a daughter. I think you were right to stop drinking, but the root reason why you used to drink is still there. You don't want to feel your emotions."

"Well, not the bad ones. Sometimes I can handle them. But when they're really bad, I have to ignore them or else they'll drown me."

"Our emotions are not something to run from. They're here for a reason. Sometimes sitting with them is all we can do."

"But they hurt. And I feel like it's going to kill me if I keep feeling that way."

"When we ignore emotions, they get more intense. The body is begging for us to release them. Let's try something. What are you feeling right now?"

"Terrified. Angry . . . Hurt."

"At whom?"

"Sarah and David. Myself."

"Let's just sit for a moment. Let those emotions be felt. We can sit in silence and feel your body and how it responds. I'll watch you to make sure they don't go too far."

"Are you sure this is a good idea?"

"I am, but we can wait if you need time."

Riley sighed. She wasn't sure if she was ready, but if it really was as simple as feeling your emotions, then she owed it to herself to at least try.

She nodded and told her to continue. Sally instructed her to close her eyes, and once she did, her feelings hit her.

Hurt coiled heavily in her stomach, burning its way through her. Her chest felt trapped under a one-hundred-pound weight, and it made her want to sink against the floor.

She sagged against the feeling, unable to fight back. This would be when she ran to a bottle or got busy with Zoe to avoid the pain she was feeling.

"Breathe through it," Sally told her.

It would have been easier to run from it, but under Sally's watch, Riley would at least see it through. The feelings burned through her, making her wince at their magnitude.

Then, they began to fade.

The weight lifted, pound by pound, until it wasn't there anymore. The hurt still swirled, but it didn't overwhelm her. It only existed.

Was this what she should have been doing all along?

Riley opened her eyes. "They're . . . they're not as bad now."

"They usually aren't once you give them the space they need."

She stared, shocked beyond all belief.

"They'll come back. Emotions aren't something that go away. We always have them. Someday, you may feel the pain again when something reminds you of David and Sarah, or you may feel it as you go to sleep, but we have to give it the space it needs, and then move on when we're ready."

"It's that easy?"

"Not easy, but it can be simple, yes. You might forget to do this, and it may get intense again. We regress, but we can always catch back up."

Riley nodded, still in a daze.

Sally glanced at the clock and told Riley they were out of time. Before she left, Sally reminded her to try the self-esteem exercise. While she hadn't talked about everything she wanted to, especially the gifting situation she kept running into with Oliver, she felt like it was more than a productive session.

Before heading out, she stopped to use the bathroom. As she washed her hands, she glanced in the mirror.

The harsh lighting did nothing for her skin, and it showed every single imperfection. She winced at the feeling of stabbing self-hatred.

But her assignment wasn't to feel that. Her assignment was to find something she *liked*.

Riley scanned her features, eyes landing on her long nose. She trailed down farther, coming up with nothing that she liked about herself.

Just as she was about to give up, she noticed it.

Her hair had streaks of gold in it. It was subtle, but her eyes caught on the shiny strands. She'd hadn't ever noticed them before. They were beautiful.

Eventually, someone came into the bathroom, and Riley jumped out of her daze. She glanced in the mirror again, eyes landing on her hair.

And she didn't hate it as much.

Riley left the therapist's office perplexed—she was exhausted from experiencing her emotions, but proud she found something she liked.

It was freeing.

She pulled out her phone and wondered if Oliver would be too busy to talk to her. She felt more like herself than she had in years, and it made sense why she did.

She remembered Thanksgiving the year before, and how she had let her anger and sadness at Amanda take over, only for it to fade when she had truly felt it. She'd done this before, only she didn't realize how important it was.

When she reflected on it, Riley had been avoiding feeling her emotions for a long time. When David cheated on her, she threw herself into taking care of Zoe. When Oliver fired her, she threw herself into working at the coffee shop. When she thought she and Oliver wouldn't work, she threw herself into Zoe's adoption.

And now her emotions were begging to be felt.

Since she had let herself feel a few of them, she was already lighter. She couldn't help the smile that brightened her face.

Her excitement was cut off by her phone ringing. She answered the moment she saw it was Oliver.

"Look across the street."

Riley frowned and did so, only to find him standing with his phone to his ear. Her jaw dropped.

"What are you doing here?" she asked as she jogged over to him.

He first pulled her into a tight hug that took her breath away. When she was finally released, her cheeks were pleasantly warm. "On lunch. My dad told me to get out of the office for a bit. I'm considering just not going back."

"That might not be a bad idea, but I don't want to discourage it too much considering it's your job."

"You're in a good mood. Did you just get out of therapy?"

"I did. I feel . . . better for once."

"That's a reason to celebrate," he said. "Let's go get food."

They wound up at a hot chicken restaurant. Oliver didn't enjoy heat very much, but Riley craved it from time to time. The place they chose was Hattie B's, which was famous in the area. It was busy, but not so much so that they couldn't find a table.

As soon as they sat, Oliver was checking his phone. He frowned, which was something he was doing more and more since Richard started.

"Is everything okay?" she asked.

"Yeah, everything's fine." He put away his phone. "Tell me about therapy."

Riley filed away his frown for later and told him about her session. He listened intently, phone lying face down on the table.

"And that's it. I need to look in the mirror to find things I like about myself and feel my emotions rather than ignoring them."

"It's a good start," he said, smiling. His phone buzzed, and the grin on his face melted into a scowl.

"What's going on? Are things really that bad where you can't have lunch every day?"

"Richard wants me to come back for a meeting," he said lowly. "I'm not going back until I've at least eaten." He took a bite of his chicken.

"How is the project going?"

"Not well. We're finding more and more people who didn't take their breaks. Well, I'm finding them. Sophie seems to be pushing them under the rug, probably on Richard's order."

"Wouldn't that make this situation worse?"

"Absolutely," he said. "Which means I'm doing the project on my own, essentially."

"Can Amanda help? She was your assistant right?"

"I . . . I don't like working with Amanda," he admitted. "I still think about how she acted when I hired you."

"It couldn't have been *that* bad. What, did she say I drank too much and couldn't handle it?"

"Yes, basically. I don't want to work directly with someone who spoke like that about you."

"She's my sister, and if she can help—"

"It wasn't okay. I'm on *your* side, Riley. As much as I respect Amanda for her work, I can't tolerate her talking about you like she does."

"Okay." Riley's cheeks were warm. When it came to Amanda and Riley, not many had taken her side in anything. Sarah used to curl Riley's hair to look like Amanda's because she thought it was cuter, and while David didn't exactly hang around with Amanda, he never defended Riley either.

"Anyway, I'm exhausted," he muttered. "I have no clue how I'm going to go back to it."

"Want some coffee? The shop isn't too far from here."

"That I will take you up on."

Riley smiled and followed Oliver to his car. They drove to the store that she managed, and she walked into a steadily busy day. Her employees were handling it well, but she made sure to check in before ordering coffee for the both of them.

In the time it took them to receive their drinks, Oliver's phone had gone off four more times.

He let out a long, pained breath. "I need to go. Riley, I'm so sorry."

She nodded. "I understand. Go."

He smiled, bending to give her a long, lingering kiss. "Thank you for being so understanding." He drove her back to her car and left shortly after.

Riley felt disappointed that she didn't get more time with him. Rather than running from that by going back to help at the shop, she sat with it for a minute.

Feeling disappointed wasn't pleasant, and while she stewed in the emotion, she fought the urge to find something else to do. But eventually, like everything else, it faded, and she felt okay.

Oliver

To say Oliver was frustrated was an understatement.

The company's lawyer had advised them not to go to the court hearings, but Richard had ignored the instruction. He'd come back angry and red in the face, telling them they all needed to find a smoking gun on the employee who was suing them. Apparently, he'd made a scene while Oliver was getting lunch, and everyone saw.

Neither Oliver nor Jack were happy.

On top of this ridiculous request, Sophie had been in the room with him all day, glancing over when she knew he was looking in her direction. She kept smiling and batting her eyelashes at him like it would make a difference in his feelings for her.

The only thing keeping him sane was the lunch with Riley and the coffee he'd gotten from her shop. He'd savored the flavor, only taking sips when he was feeling particularly murderous.

Eventually, after six, Richard stormed out, saying he was going to a bar and would come back tomorrow with some damning evidence. Oliver doubted that.

Jack looked exhausted, and Oliver was sure he looked about the same.

He wanted to get home to Riley. He didn't want to look at another person in a suit for a week.

But he had to come back the very next morning.

He exited the meeting room in a rush. He grabbed his long since empty cup, planning on throwing it away before going to his car.

"That place is *so* good."

He sighed. Sophie had followed him.

He turned to her. "What do you want?"

"I was just saying that coffee shop is good." She pointed to the empty cup in his hands. "I remember when we used to get coffee."

He doubted Sophie had ever been to where Riley worked. If she had and Riley saw her, she would have told him.

And besides, when he and Sophie used to get coffee, they only went to large chains. He had nothing against those, but it wasn't as good as where Riley worked.

"We would go on dates and hold hands," she said, stepping closer to him. He stepped back. "It was so romantic."

"We're at work. You know I don't do this in the office."

Sophie pouted. "Not even for me?"

"No, not even for you." The only person he'd ever broken his rules for was Riley. "I will not be having this conversation. It's been a long day, and I want to go home."

"I don't blame you. It's such a pretty house, and so close to the office . . ."

Oliver cringed. He'd momentarily forgotten that Sophie knew where he lived. Thankfully, the security guards knew better than to let her in, but he hated that she had even seen his home, been a part of his life.

"I'm leaving."

"It must be so hard going home alone."

"I'm not alone," he muttered, thinking of Riley and Zoe.

He shook his head and walked off, but he could feel her eyes on him, watching him as he left. It tightened the muscles in his back in an unpleasant way.

Maybe he needed to let HR know about this. They were busy with the court case and finding replacements for all the people who had quit, but this wasn't something he needed to be dealing with at work. With him in a position of power, and with the ever-worsening court case, he needed to be careful with what he did or said. He could easily stir the office-gossip pot.

If HR stepped in, more people would know about his life. But he was also tired of dealing with it. After all, she was making advances after he'd said no.

When he got home, he wondered if Riley was still disappointed he couldn't stay longer at their impromptu lunch. She'd been understanding, but her smile hadn't reached her eyes.

Walking in, he was surprised to see that Zoe was in her room playing. She smiled when he went up to check on her, but said she wanted to play by herself after being around other kids all day. While Oliver understood, he also missed his daughter.

"Hey," Riley said from her seated spot on the floor of the living room as he came down the stairs. She looked to be organizing Zoe's mess of toys which were spread all over the floor. As much as Oliver wanted to help, all he could do was flop onto the couch.

"Bad day?" she asked.

"Terrible. Richard wants to go after the employee's character to try and find out if she lied."

"Is that allowed?"

"Technically, our lawyer said we could do our own research, but it isn't what my dad and I want to do. We spent the day trying to talk Richard off the ledge only for him to nail himself down onto it. Needless to say, we didn't get anywhere."

"I'm sorry," Riley said. "That's a lot."

"Thank you for taking care of Zoe," he added. "I really cannot thank you enough for cutting some of your hours at the shop to be able to get her from the school."

"It's no problem. I let her run free while I did some work from here anyway. That's why the house is a disaster."

"I don't even care," he said with a heavy groan. "I'm just glad I wasn't sitting at work worried that she wasn't happy. Those first four years when I didn't have anyone were tough. I don't know what I would do if I still was in that position."

"Well, you're not. And she was happy. You don't have to thank me, though. This is all part of being a parent, and I knew what I was signing up for when I decided to adopt her."

Oliver still couldn't believe it. She had taken on the role so perfectly, never once asking for anything in return for being Zoe's mom. She didn't want him for his money, or even his house. She was here because Zoe was here, but he didn't doubt that she would be present even if she lived somewhere else.

The bond that Riley and Zoe had was something he'd only ever dreamed of. Sophie had treated Zoe like a chore she couldn't be bothered to do. Riley treated Zoe like a gift.

At the thought of his ex, Oliver sighed again.

"Anything you want to talk about?" Riley asked.

"It's nothing you'll enjoy hearing," he told her. "It's Sophie."

"Did she do something?" Her voice went hard.

"Nothing more than we expected. She's using this as a way to get back with me."

Riley frowned.

"Not that I ever will," he rushed to assure her. "I don't see her that way."

"I know," she said, "but I can image this is how you felt when David cornered me that day in the parking lot."

He remembered that, even though it had been before they dated. David had tried to rekindle things with Riley when he had broken it off with Sarah. Later, Riley discovered that he was trying to get back with both of them, and Sarah was the one who caved first.

"I should put in something with HR," he said. "But it's a weird situation, considering I'm her boss and I technically have the power over her. Not that I want to use it. I've mainly been avoiding her."

"When does she do this?"

"When she follows me out."

"Can Jack leave with you?"

"He's been just as swamped as me. Usually, he leaves later. This whole situation with the lawsuit and then Sophie being on the project has made things so difficult."

Riley frowned, looking angry, but then she closed her eyes and didn't speak for a moment. When she opened them, she seemed calmer.

He watched her in wonder.

"I trust you," she said. "I don't trust her."

"She can't do much at work. If she touches me, I can have her fired."

Riley nodded. "Do what you can."

"Always," he said, and he meant it.

There was a knock on the door, and Riley moved to stand.

"I've got it," he told her.

"Are you sure?"

"Yeah." He slowly rose from the couch and answered the door.

He barely recognized the woman, but she was dressed in a neatly pressed Chanel dress. She held a clipboard with papers and smiled at him in the same way Sophie used to.

"Mr. Brian. I'm Kyla Jensen. I live two doors down and am the head of the HOA."

"Hi, Kyla," he said flatly. He wondered if this was the same woman who had insinuated Riley she was a gold digger.

"I won't take much of your time, but I wanted to invite you to the board meeting for the neighborhood. We're thinking about making some big changes."

"I don't know if I'll have time, but maybe Riley would be interested."

"Riley," she said, her smile fading a bit. "Your nanny?"

"No, my girlfriend. She lives here too."

"I didn't realize you were with anyone. She must have been the woman I saw with your daughter at school. I was *so* worried. I know how protective you are of your child."

"I am. Riley is amazing with her."

"She must be a lucky woman, being involved with someone as successful as you."

"I would consider myself the lucky one," he replied, glancing at the ring on her finger.

"That's very sweet of you to say."

It was then Oliver heard footsteps.

"I'm sorry," Zoe was saying. "I didn't mean to spill the water you gave me."

"It's okay," Riley replied, sounding in no way bothered. "Let's get a towel and clean it up together.

Oliver's chest warmed at the sight. She didn't even look at the door. She was so focused on Zoe that she headed right to the kitchen, staying on task.

He turned back to his neighbor. Kyla's eyes were on where Riley disappeared, and she frowned.

"As you can see," he said, "I really am the lucky one. I'll give her the information. Maybe you'll see her there."

Oliver slowly shut the door after taking a flyer from Kyla. Riley may be interested in knowing more about the neighborhood, but he highly doubted she would if Kyla were there.

He set it on the dining room table and then went to check on Riley and Zoe's progress with cleanup.

They were almost done with it.

After reiterating the stance that Zoe wasn't in trouble, he followed Riley down the stairs.

"What was that about?" she asked. "I think I recognized that voice."

"That was a neighbor named Kyla."

Riley shrugged. "Doesn't ring a bell."

"I have a feeling she is the neighbor that you ran into at the school. She left a flyer. I put it on the dining room table."

Riley walked to the dining room, grabbing the paper with a frown.

"An HOA meeting?" she asked.

"You don't have to go. I think it was a way of trying to connect with me."

"What did her ring look like? Could you ice skate on it?"

"It was . . . rather huge. I'd say four or five carats."

"I know nothing about carats, but what I do know is it could be seen from space."

"That's the one."

Riley rolled her eyes, then looked down at the paper. "The flyer says she wants to make the neighborhood more family friendly. If it was the woman I saw, I highly doubt she came by because of HOA matters." Riley threw it in the trash.

"You handled that well," he said. "I know it must be weird to have a neighbor do that."

"It is weird, but it's no weirder than the situation with Sophie. I'm not *that* worried about it. I'm not wasting time that I have with you at home thinking about that stuff."

She smiled at him, appearing and sounding more like herself than she had in a long time, and he couldn't look away. Camilla had been right. Riley rose to the challenge of fixing herself. Just as always, she did it with far more grace than he ever could.

Chapter Eight

Riley

For a few weeks, things were quiet.

Well, as quiet as they could be.

Riley's therapy sessions went well. Though, she felt like she was so busy working on herself and taking care of Zoe she didn't have a moment to spare. The weather cooled sometime in October. Cooler weather meant the coffee shop was packed with people wanting their favorite seasonal drink, which made the shop smell of chai spices, hazelnut, and sweet maple. Riley was needed more and more at the business, making her lean on her mother far more than she normally would to look after Zoe.

The only person busier than Riley was Oliver. He was in the office from early morning hours to well after dark, so most of the housework fell to her. Luckily, the whole family was out of the house so much that it didn't get very messy, but Oliver still thanked her for taking on things whenever he saw her.

What free time he had went to her and Zoe. He always found time to ask how therapy was going and how she felt about it. She usually had the same answers. It was fine, and it was going well. She was doing what work she could on herself, but it was slow. Each meeting was chipping away at a mountain of trauma and pain. She was tired, but that meant she was getting it done.

So far, when she looked in the mirror, she'd found five things about herself that she liked. It was progress.

Riley and Sally were still digging into how David treated her when they were together. While she didn't want to remember how stupid she was to stay with him, Sally had assured her multiple times that she wasn't dumb—Riley had trusted David, and he'd taken advantage of that.

Sally kept reiterating for Riley to observe, to see how her current relationship differed from her past one.

Oliver was the polar opposite. He was busy, and yet still made time to listen to her more than David ever did. Even though he had infinitely more responsibility than David, he still found time for both of them. One day in therapy, she had admitted that she wouldn't blame him if he focused solely on Zoe. After all, she was the priority.

But he never did. When Zoe was awake, he spent time with her. And then after their child was in bed, his attention was focused on Riley.

They talked about their days. They talked about therapy, about their pasts. Sometimes, they simply watched movies in each other's presence.

And it was nice.

Slowly, she was learning to trust again. She and Sally identified and deconstructed the red flags David had presented, and when she looked to her current relationship, they weren't there. Oliver wasn't distant. He didn't make odd comments about other women the way David did.

And she was figuring out he was maybe actually committed, and maybe they would work.

"What are you thinking about over there?" Oliver asked, pulling her out of her musings.

It was late. Zoe was asleep and he had gotten home at six instead of the late nights they were all used to. Riley was cleaning up after dinner when she zoned out, thinking about all the ways things seemed to be right for once.

"Just something I learned in therapy."

Oliver raised his eyebrows.

She put down the rag she had been wiping the counter with. "It's not much, but we've been working on me seeing the red flags of my past relationships. Not in a way where I'm beating myself up over anything, just seeing why things ended up the way they did, and how the present isn't the same."

"How is it not the same?"

Riley laughed. "What—are you fishing for compliments or something?"

"I want to hear how you see it, and if I get a compliment I won't complain," he said.

She sighed and hopped up to sit on the counter. Her sore feet thanked her.

"David was distant," she explained. "I had normalized it. When I came home, I was used to him playing his video games or ignoring me. I'd have to beg him to run a bath. The night he cheated, I had broken up a bar fight and gotten punched—"

"What?" Oliver said, shocked.

"Not directly. I tried to break it up and was in the cross fire."

"Still. That was—"

"That right there," she said, pointing to his expression, "that concern? David never had that. If I had been lucky, he would have gotten shit-faced with me and *maybe* run me a bath."

"I'm so glad you quit that job," he said darkly. "I can't believe you got hit at work."

"In hindsight, it was scarier than I realized. I met you only a few days later. I wore my flannel the whole day because the bruise was still visible."

He walked over to her, standing between her legs. "Have I ever told you I am so glad you worked for me?" His hand trailed up her thigh and she lost her words for a moment.

"You have," she said. "And I am too. I've been realizing that things are so different now."

"That bar was terrible, and if anyone ever does that to you again—"

"The only person is Zoe, and I think she can get away with it." She tried to play it cool, but her body felt hot at his protection. This was what she never had before. This was the reason she wanted to trust again.

Oliver kissed along her jaw and moved to her neck. She hummed. "Should we move to the bedroom?"

"Yes, but maybe just to sleep." Oliver laid his head on her shoulder. "I am so tired."

"You tease," she said.

"Sorry, should I not kiss you if I'm tired?"

She tapped her chin as she playfully thought about it. "I guess I'll allow it, but only if I get to lay on your shoulder this time. The last time you laid on me I thought I was going to die."

Oliver returned the laugh. "Fine, but we're taking turns."

"We'll see about that," she said, and followed him to their bedroom.

The next morning, Riley was working behind the counter at the shop when she saw someone walk in that she'd rather not see.

Sophie.

She knew this was always a possibility. As the coffee shop grew, so did the chances that a familiar face would walk in. So far, Riley had seen three people she knew from high school, one guy she'd gone on a few dates with, and a few celebrities. She was out in the front so often that she knew it was just part of the job.

However, there would always be people she dreaded seeing.

Sophie's eyes roamed the shop with disinterest. Riley wondered if Oliver had let it slip that Riley worked here, but she knew from Amanda that he had held true to his rule of not talking about his personal life at work.

Riley gritted her teeth and knew there was no way for Sophie to not spot her. She was working behind the line, busy with drinks, but she was also close enough to the front to be able to help the newer employee if they needed it.

Sure enough, Sophie's eyes trailed over to Riley, and the other woman did a double take, eyes wide.

Huh. So, Sophie *didn't* know she worked here.

Sophie immediately trained on to her like a lion watching its prey. Riley blushed and continued making drinks. She could probably kick Sophie out if she wanted to, but she needed a reason first. It wasn't exactly good customer service to remove someone just because there's bad blood from the past.

Even if Riley wanted to kick Sophie in the shins.

She walked up, eyes still focused on Riley. She waited in line, but Riley knew there would be questions the instant she was up at the counter.

Ugh.

When it was finally Sophie's turn to order, she gave the employee at the register a wide, fake smile and asked, "Do you do catering orders?"

The cashier instantly looked at Riley with wide eyes.

"Depends on if our supplier can swing it," she answered, gesturing for someone to take her station. She ignored her racing heart and tried to put on her best customer-facing smile. "What do you need?"

Sophie laughed incredulously. "Do you own the place or something?"

"In a way," Riley said. "I'm the manager on duty, and I'm the one that can tell you whether we can do the catering order or not. What do you need?"

"How did you go from being a nanny to a manager in the span of less than a year?"

"I like to work," she replied flatly. "You mentioned a catering order?"

"Yes, well, I need to cater some coffee and cinnamon rolls to my office. It's been so stressful, and I want to do something nice for my bosses."

"Aw," the cashier said.

Riley resisted the urge to roll her eyes. Having to cater an order not only to Sophie, but to Oliver's company, and then have to be complicit in Sophie's plan to woo him was not her idea of a fun afternoon.

However, she could upcharge the shit out of this. Catering was something they were just starting, but it had the potential to be profitable.

Very profitable.

"How much do you need?" Riley grabbed a notepad from behind the register. "I'll see if I can make it happen."

Oliver

Oliver was enjoying a quiet moment alone when he received a message from the office manager that made him pause.

It was an announcement that there was a surprise refreshments in the break room, and it was from Riley's coffee shop, of all places.

Since Richard had started, the company drastically reduced the number of free meals or catering they offered the employees. It was all a part of his money-saving scheme, but Oliver himself missed the times where he could see more of his employees happily eating something the company provided.

This announcement about something Richard had been so proud to squash caught him off guard, but it being from Riley's coffee shop was throwing him for a loop.

He walked to the break room where he saw Sophie and Richard talking. She immediately saw him and walked over. Richard followed.

"I'm really glad you convinced me to let this happen, Sophie," Richard said in between bites of a gooey, flaky cinnamon roll. "This stuff is good."

"It's Oliver's favorite place!" Sophie exclaimed. "Surprise!"

Oliver gaped. He had never said it was his favorite, though it was because Riley worked there.

"Uh, what?" he asked. "Isn't this an extraneous purchase since we're supposed to be financially tightening our belts?"

"Oh, come on." Sophie reached for him, and he stepped away. "This is for you! We've all been working so hard, and I saw you had coffee from the shop, so I had them bring in coffee and snacks. There's a lot of cinnamon rolls left."

"I think I'm going to have a third," Richard said, finishing the last of what was in his hand.

"What location did you order this from?" Oliver asked.

"Oh, the one not too far from here. You'll never guess who I ran into."

Oh no. She'd definitely seen Riley.

That was when Riley turned the corner. She was wearing jeans and a T-shirt with a logo of the coffee shop. She was chatting with Amanda, who had coffee and a cinnamon roll in hand.

Seeing her in his work environment made his heart flip. He was so used to seeing her only at home, or at the café, and recently, that hadn't been enough.

"Oh," Sophie said, frowning. "*She's* here."

"Amanda is her sister."

Riley's eyes caught his, and she gave him a beautiful, but tired, smile. Oliver stepped away from Sophie and approached Amanda and Riley.

"Hey," he said. "So, this was a surprise."

"Yeah, but catering is where the money is," Riley said, shrugging. "She came in this morning and asked. Our supplier was able to pull it off. Barely. I charged your company a lot of money, though."

"That's fair. This wasn't my idea, by the way. Apparently, Richard approved it."

"Which one is that?"

"Balding guy," Amanda interjected. "He's a real piece of work."

Oliver shouldn't be hearing this, but he couldn't help but nod. Amanda smirked. "Glad you agree, Oliver."

"I should get going," Riley said. "Judging by the way the Wicked Witch of the West is glaring over here, I'm about to attacked by a bunch of winged monkeys."

Amanda laughed. "Yeah, how is that going anyway?" She glanced at Oliver and he sighed.

"It's mainly her trying to talk to me, and me constantly walking away."

Amanda looked genuinely surprised he answered, and he didn't blame her. He was always tight-lipped within the walls of the office.

But then again, Riley was here, and he'd always been bad about running his mouth in her presence.

"You know," Riley said, crossing her arms, "I could accidentally spill one of the gallons of hot coffee I just brought in. Who do you want it to be on? Sophie or Richard?"

He laughed. "I refuse to be a part of this, but I won't stop you."

Amanda looked in between them with the same confused expression she always did when he would joke in her presence. He still struggled with finding a balance between being the mum CFO of her company and her almost brother-in-law.

"Oh," Amanda said, her eyes landing behind them. "Sophie alert. That's my cue to leave."

Amanda darted away as Oliver and Riley turned in time to see Sophie walking up to them. He was torn between grabbing his girlfriend's hand and wanting to keep her at arm's length as the caterer.

"Wow, Riley. I didn't know you would be the one delivering." Sophie smiled, but her eyes were narrowed.

"I wanted it to go well, and there's no better way to ensure that than to do it myself."

That was Riley's mantra with many things.

"You must be so busy," she said. "I bet you have loads to get back to."

Out of nowhere, the office manager, Taylor, piped in. "Oh!" She walked over with a smile on her face. "You must be the delivery person. Wow, your shop is so good."

Sophie frowned at the intrusion, but Oliver guessed it was mainly because it made Riley stay longer.

"It's my friend's shop, but thank you. I'll pass on your compliment."

"It's hers too," Oliver added. "She's an investor."

"Wow," Sophie said, her voice louder than Oliver wanted. "How did you go from being Oliver's nanny to a coffee shop *investor*?"

People paused, and Oliver tensed. Everyone wanted a piece of his life, especially because he was so quiet about it, and now, they were about to get it.

"I saved money and worked my ass off," Riley said, her voice just as tense. "I actually spent less time trying to sleep with my boss and more time working. You should take that advice."

Taylor's jaw dropped, and so did half the room. Sophie went pale, but Oliver couldn't be prouder of Riley. She'd said the perfect thing—not naming him, but painting Sophie to be the person she truly was.

"I need to head out," Riley added. "I'm glad everything turned out well." She started to walk away, but Oliver, spurred on by her bravery, grabbed her hand.

"I love you," he said genuinely. "I'll see you at home?"

He could practically hear the gossip-wheels turning.

Riley smiled fully at him, the one that made his heart stop. "Yeah, of course. I love you too, Oliver."

Her eyes flickered to his lips, but she didn't move to kiss him, as if unsure if it was okay to do it at his place of work.

Oliver made that decision for her. Her stepped forward, putting a steady hand on her hip, and brought her in for a kiss. Despite the eyes on them, her scent mixed with coffee filled his nose and brought him a sense of peace.

When he pulled away, her cheeks were slightly pink, but her smile was bright and full. She left without another word and he watched her go, purposefully ignoring the shocked looks of his employees.

Face aflame, he quickly retreated to his office the second he could. He'd really done it this time.

He got a few hours of blessed silence to finish some of his work before he messaged Taylor to see if there were any refreshments left. She replied she had saved some for him. He exited his office only to find Sophie was waiting for him beside Amanda's old desk.

Oliver had no idea how long she'd waited, but she looked annoyed. If he still had an assistant, Sophie wouldn't have been able to ambush him.

"You're dating your nanny?" Sophie asked, her voice low.

He was surprised at her change in tone. Usually, she tried to appear so sweet to him, but this must have been her true self.

"Former. And yes," he said.

"You stooped that low for her?"

"I stooped low? What—because she doesn't wear flashy jewelry and isn't after me for my money? You hated Riley the moment you saw her, and we both know it was because you saw her as a threat."

"She was your nanny, Oliver."

"Yeah. She used to work for me. And you do too," he said. "It's not that different."

"How do you know she's not after your money? You see how she dresses. She's poor."

"Why would I care how much money she has? She treats Zoe like her own."

"I treated Zoe like my own."

"Then you definitely should not become a parent. Now, if you'll excuse me, I'm going to the break room."

Oliver started to walk away, but Sophie wasn't finished. "Everyone knows you're dating her now, Oliver. You have to hate that."

"Here's the thing, Sophie," he began, "I don't care if everyone knows, because I'm not ashamed of her. I may hate that people know about my personal life, but I bet you hate it more that Riley called you out for what you are to your face."

"Are you this cruel to your daughter?" she asked, voice almost quaking with anger.

"No, only to people who hurt my daughter," he said. "You should go find Richard. I'm sure he has something for you to do."

He finally walked away and was able to retrieve his leftover cinnamon roll without anyone asking about his love life. Once he returned to his office, he ate and continued working, up until Jack told them all that there was an urgent meeting.

He sighed. Time to go see whatever this was about. He hoped it was good news, at least.

It was, unfortunately, not good news.

"It is looking like the judge will side with the employee," Jack announced. His barely contained fury had Oliver thankful it wasn't directed at him. "The policy was too strict and is considered a workplace violation."

"This is bullshit!" Richard snapped. "Our employees shouldn't be so stupid."

"Don't speak about employees like that," Oliver butted in. "Many of them have come forward about the changes to the working conditions here. They felt pressure to skip legally mandated breaks. The productivity standards you set are too high for them to be able to hit every week. The best option is to reverse those policies and settle. This is your fault, Richard."

"You're blaming the one who saved you millions of dollars?"

"Millions we will be paying in a settlement," Jack added. "Not to mention the damage to our otherwise good reputation."

"The investors wanted me in here for a reason."

Oliver glanced at his father. He and Jack were definitely bringing all of this to the investors' attention. They had concrete proof Richard had put the company at financial risk with his policies.

But he couldn't know they were coming for him, so Oliver would have to keep a lid on his anger for now.

From the chair she inexplicably had in the executive-only meeting, Sophie said, "Well, I think we can all agree we're tired of this."

She didn't look at Oliver and seemed to be still fuming from his earlier dismissal.

Good.

"I'm done with being blamed for everything," Richard said. "I'm leaving."

He confidently strode out of the office. Sophie glared at him and did the same. Oliver shook his head after they were gone.

"That was absolutely ridiculous," he said.

"I want the investors on the phone," Jack said. "Now."

He could tell his father meant business, and they locked the room doors and corralled all the investors into a meeting.

It was going to be a long day, but he couldn't bring himself to mind. If they settled and got the investors to approve Richard's dismissal, then it would all be worth it.

Many hours later, he was finally heading home after listening to his father yell at investors for hours. He was exhausted but felt energized when they finally agreed to sign off on letting Richard go.

This massive project and lawsuit was now over—at least the parts he needed to oversee, anyway.

It was dark outside, and the lights in the house were off.

There was food in the microwave and a note from Riley saying she'd cooked. It was after nine, so he had once again missed out on time with Zoe; but soon, things would be changing. He could finally be home more.

Oliver drank a glass of water and ate dinner. The house was quiet and dark, a sad reminder of how long he'd been at the office.

Eventually, he headed to his and Riley's bedroom. The shower was running, and he opened the door.

The room was enveloped in the scent of peony and jasmine, which had quickly become his favorite scent.

"Hey," he said.

He could see her outline jump in the shower. "Fuck, Oliver. Don't scare me like that."

"Sorry," he said, laughing. "Mind if I join you?"

It was a rare time when he could shower when she did. Even rarer that Zoe was asleep during those times.

"Sure," she said. "I have the water scalding, though."

"I don't doubt it." The weather was beginning to cool, and he knew she was already freezing.

He peeled off his work clothes, his body stiff from his day. He opened the frosted glass door, taking a moment to admire Riley's naked form before he climbed in.

"This wasn't as hot as I thought you'd have it," he said, the water spraying his back.

"Maybe I'm converting you," she said with a smile. "Being boiled alive is fun."

He grabbed her bare hips and pulled her toward him, kissing her softly. While they'd had sex more often than any of his other relationships, his increased workload and Riley's increased stress meant most nights were just for sleep.

Now that the case was over, and therapy was making her seem more herself, his body was *alive*.

Plus, she was literally naked in front of him. He couldn't think about anything else.

He kissed her slowly but surely. The scent of her bodywash enveloped him, and he felt himself burn as her body pressed against his. Riley moaned softly. He could feel himself rapidly hardening, despite how exhausted his day made him.

"You're so beautiful," he mumbled, pushing her against the wet wall. He kissed her again, his tongue entering her open mouth.

"Aren't you tired from your day?" She panted as his mouth found its way to her neck.

They had an unspoken agreement. If one of them mentioned how tired they were, sex was off the table. And even though he could definitely use the sleep, he knew his body wouldn't let him, not until he got to feel her.

"Not at this moment. I want you too much." His hand trailed down to grab her ass. "Do you want this too?"

"Yes," she said immediately, running her fingers through his wet hair and bringing him back down to her mouth.

Eager to hear the sounds of her pleasure, he moved his hand to her front, pressing his fingers against her wet center.

Oliver was tempted to push a finger inside her and feel her warmth, but he wanted her shaking for him first. He made long strokes with his fingers, from her clit to her entrance, something that always had her gazing with desire.

"Fuck, Oliver . . ." She was completely lost in sensation. He loved it when she talked to him—when she told him what she liked. It only made him want to give her more of it.

Riley leaned heavily on the tile of the shower wall, opening herself up to him more. At the end of his strokes, his fingers would barely dip into her before returning the attention to her center, circling it before going back.

Her grip on his shoulder's tightened, and he could hear her breaths coming faster. She began to work her hips against his fingers, and he gave her more of the friction she needed.

Her shocked gasps intermingled with pleasure as her body released. He dipped one finger inside of her as the orgasm rippled throughout and could feel her core tightening.

When she was finished, she pulled him to her, pressing her lips to his insistently. Her tongue made its way into his mouth, and he still kept his fingers inside of her as they roughly kissed.

"Fuck me," she said as he pulled his fingers away.

His cock jerked at the invitation.

"I could," he offered, "but I could also go down on you until you pass out."

Her cheeks darkened at the offer, but she shook her head. "I want you," she said. "Don't you want me to cum on your cock?"

The words were enough to make him lose his concentration, so he turned her around and angled her to where he could press himself against her entrance.

One day, a little voice in the back of his head said, one day you'll be able to convince her to let you spoil her. In every way.

But her moans in the moment told him she also wanted to be fucked. And who was he to say no?

"Oliver," she whined. "Come on. Fuck me."

He didn't need to be told again.

He pressed the head of his cock in, her warmth almost making him lose control, but he knew she loved this part. She loved to be teased, and her soft moans told him this was no exception.

He pulled out once, taking a moment to rub himself against her sensitive clit. He got his reward when she gasped and jerked against him. Then he went back to her entrance, pressing in even more.

He did this several more times, working her up to the edge of another orgasm. She was whimpering and gasping, rocking against him no matter where he was.

Then he was done waiting.

When the head of his cock reached her again, he plunged inside, filling her completely.

"Oh, God. Yes, Oliver!" she moaned. He took only one moment to feel her tightness encasing his shaft. Then he began to move, thrusting into her with more and more force. He had her hips in a tight grip as he completely lost control.

She was vocal, making a sound with each thrust, her hips moving in tandem with his. He could feel himself building as he plunged into her over and over.

What broke him was a stuttered moan from her, and the tightening of her core around him as she came again. Her second orgasms were always better than the first, and he'd always wondered what her third, fourth, or fifth would be like.

Oliver groaned and spilled into her. Her pussy milked every drop from him, and he rutted into her as his orgasm continued. He loved this feeling of nothing in between them, and the sight of his own cum leaking out of her as he finally pulled out.

The water had gone cold, and neither of them noticed. He felt spent, both from his day and from finally getting to fuck her like he wanted to.

She pulled him into a kiss, and he wished he wasn't so tired, because the idea of a round two wasn't so bad.

"That was amazing," she said, out of breath. "But now I need some sleep."

"Me too," he admitted tiredly. He let her dry him off and followed as she led them to bed. Oliver was asleep as soon as his head hit the pillow.

Chapter Nine

Riley

Riley woke up gently, feeling the pleasant sensation of the morning after sex. As usual, her body was sated and relaxed, with the touch of the welcome ache that reminded her of their surprisingly intimate shower.

He was already awake and she could hear the chaos of a morning with Zoe. It was Wednesday, which meant it was her day to take her to school. She slowly got up, stretching out her tightened body. She got dressed and left the bedroom to see Zoe was already ready to go.

"I'll take her in today," Oliver said, kissing her on the forehead.

"But it's my day to do it."

"I know, but I've missed so much time with her lately. I'd love to do it."

"Well, I can't say no to a relaxing morning by myself," she mused. She had work and therapy today, neither of which were going to be easy.

"I made coffee," he said. "Zoe, are you ready to go?"

"Can we get cinnamon rolls?" Zoe asked as she put on her backpack. She gave Riley a hug before her attention was back on her father.

"What happened to the three eggs you just ate?"

"I'm still hungry."

"Fine, I *suppose* we could swing by our favorite coffee shop." He glanced at Riley.

"The shift leader on duty today knows who you are," she replied. "Get as much as you want."

She smiled as they left. With Oliver being so busy, he and Zoe hadn't had much time together. Recently, Riley had been Zoe's favorite, but once the newness of the adoption wore off, she wanted her dad too.

Zoe loved Riley, but Oliver's business life had consumed a lot of all three of their lives. Whenever he had the time, she expected Zoe to be attached to him rather than her.

She received a notification on her phone, which wound up being a voicemail from her gynecologist's office. She usually had notifications off in the morning so she could focus on getting Zoe to school.

Apparently, there was an issue where her insurance wasn't covering the birth control implant. She groaned, knowing she still had her pill refill that she had picked up not too long ago, but she kept forgetting to take it, especially while she and Oliver were so busy.

She called her insurance, and they asked for so much information that the call took twenty minutes. When she finally got them to agree to cover it, her fingers were tapping against the counter in annoyance.

Now she had to go to therapy in a sour mood. She *hated* dealing with insurance. After fuming for a few minutes, she rummaged through her closet to see if she still had a box of Plan B in her things. She tried to keep one box in her possession at all times just in case she forgot to take her birth control and she and Oliver had sex.

She probably hadn't taken it regularly enough for it to work.

After no luck in her closet, she was close to being late for her appointment. She checked Oliver's nightstand, just in case she hid them in a place Zoe wouldn't find them.

That was when she saw it.

Riley didn't know why he would have a pamphlet from a jeweler with rings circled. She didn't know if this was left over from when he was dating Sophie, or if this was for her. She frowned as she looked at the rings. Unless Oliver was totally blind to Sophie's taste, these were *not* her style. They looked . . . simple. More like something Riley would wear.

Holy *shit*. Was he about to propose? To *her*?

Maybe Riley should have planned for it. After all, Oliver was the kind of guy who moved fast. Then again, there was no rush. She was Zoe's mom now. Wasn't that why he wanted a wife?

And if so, why her?

She backpedaled on the thought, dimly remembering Sally's advice. She didn't need to question his decision. If he wanted to marry her, her only question should be would she want to say yes.

And for that—Riley had no idea.

Oliver was the perfect boyfriend. She was so lucky to have him. But a marriage?

Riley put the pamphlet back where it belonged and closed the drawer. She pressed her hands against her face, trying to cool the warm skin.

She needed to get to therapy. Maybe Sally would have some good insight into this.

"How are you today?" Sally asked.

"Oliver's planning to propose," Riley said quickly. She had thought about it all in the car, turning over this new information like a stone in her mind.

Nothing came up.

"Wow. How are you feeling?"

"No clue. I'm scared, and my instant reaction is to say I don't deserve it. That means I'm not ready, right?"

"Not necessarily. Do you think you're not ready?"

"Maybe? I never thought about it. He always mentioned marrying someone to give Zoe a mom, but he doesn't have to do that with me."

"Perhaps he has other reasons then."

Riley blushed. The idea that he wanted to marry her for no other benefit than her companionship was hard for her to accept. She still struggled with seeing herself as so much less than him that it never occurred to her how *he* saw her. She'd managed to continue her self-esteem building exercise, but it was always a struggle to look past the things she didn't like in order to find the new ones she did.

"How do *you* feel about marriage?" Sally asked.

Riley blinked. "I wanted it when I was younger. It felt like the next step to everything. But then David always said we shouldn't."

"And what about marriage with Oliver?"

"I love him," she replied honestly. "I look forward to seeing him when he comes home, and I like spending time with him."

"Do you plan on leaving him?"

"No." She shook her head. "I don't. If we ever ended . . . I always thought he would be the one to do it."

"This seems to be evidence to the contrary."

"Exactly, and logically, it makes sense. We love each other and we're committed, but . . ."

"It *is* a big step."

"I'm terrified. This could mean I would be listed as the owner of a house that I could never afford. I'd be tied to him. I don't know if he wants to share a bank account, and the idea of having access to that much money scares me."

"You don't have to make these decisions now. Many couples have many different ways of joining their lives. Some have separate accounts, some don't. It's up to you to decide what you want, to set the boundaries with what you're comfortable with."

"Right. I used to want marriage with David because I thought it would mean we would share our lives. He always kept so many secrets about where his money was going and why he needed extra money for rent . . . I never wanted that after we got married."

"It doesn't seem like you have those issues with Oliver."

"No," Riley said, laughing. "I don't think he would *ever* need money from me, which is still so weird to me. I've asked about finances, and he always answers honestly. He's never lied to me about anything."

"So you don't need marriage for that. What if I told you that marriage can simply be something you want, and not something you *need* to do?"

"I'd agree, and then I'd wonder where I got the idea that it was anything else."

"We all forget what things mean sometimes, but the question remains: what do *you* want?"

"I . . . want to marry him."

Sally smiled. "Then you have your answer."

Oliver

Heading home from work when the sun was up was strange, but Oliver was grateful. Now that he and Jack knew they were going to settle this case and Steph in HR was drawing up paperwork to fire Richard, there was less urgent work to be done; it could all wait for the morning.

When he got home, Riley and Zoe were debating dinner. Zoe wanted to go to McDonald's, which was her new favorite place. Riley hated fast food ever since she stopped drinking. She said it reminded her of David too much.

"What about that Mexican place?" Riley asked. "The one with the fountain."

"No," Zoe said. "I want a burger. A McDonald's burger."

Riley rubbed her face. "What about a burger from somewhere else? There's that place with the playground."

"The one with milkshakes?" Zoe asked hopefully.

Riley groaned. "Yes, that one."

"Can I have a milkshake?"

"You know what? Fine, as long as it gets us food."

"Yes!" It was then the little girl noticed him. "Daddy!" she exclaimed as she ran to give him a hug.

"Hey, Zoe," he said, smiling and hugging her back.

"You're home before five?" Riley asked.

"Since we've decided to settle and Richard is about to get fired, the workload is lighter for once."

"I've never been so glad to hear that your company lost money," Riley said with a chuckle. She glanced in the direction of the bedroom, and her smile fell a bit.

"How was therapy?" he asked.

"Um, fine," she replied, but she sounded a bit uncertain. "How was your day?"

He narrowed his eyes.

"Fine, we talked about . . . the future," she settled on. "It wasn't a bad conversation or anything."

"I want food!" Zoe called.

"I heard we're having burgers," Oliver said. Riley looked grateful for the distraction, but he wasn't done with this conversation. He'd ask her about it later. "I can take Zoe out if you need some time to unwind."

"I'm not staying here when I can finally have dinner with my family. Let's go."

They drove to a local burger place with a diner feel and a small playground. It was packed, but local places in Nashville usually were.

Zoe forgot about food quickly when she saw other kids playing. She immediately joined in, playing big sister to half of the little kids being left out by the older ones.

"She's great with younger kids," Riley said, crossing her arms.

"Surprisingly. It's so strange since Luke and Landon are both older."

"I think she likes being the oldest," she said with a smile. "Let's find a table."

He nodded and chose to sit beside Riley and leave the rest of the booth open for Zoe to run in an out. She would play until food was in her sights.

Oliver immediately knew what he wanted. They frequented this restaurant all the time when neither of them felt like cooking. Zoe had mentioned it many times while he was working late. He wondered how much Riley had spent at this place.

Maybe he should pay her back.

"So," Riley started. Her menu was folded, and he guessed she had decided quickly too. "The future . . . any new thoughts on kids?"

He raised an eyebrow. "We're going there before even getting appetizers?"

She shrugged. "You're curious about therapy, and I'm straight to the point."

"So, you talked about kids?"

"Kind of," she said. "I can tell you're avoiding the question."

"I haven't had time," he said, sighing. "But no. I really doubt I'll change my mind on it."

"Was Zoe's first year that bad?"

"Zoe had this thing where she cried nonstop. My dad was basically doing my job for the first year of Zoe's life because I couldn't get any work done. When I did finally make it to work, she hated all of her nannies, until you."

"That does sound hard, but I didn't get to experience that with Zoe. I don't think I could agree to *never* having more. Now that I'm thinking about it, I think I'd want a big family."

She was asking for the one thing Oliver might not be able to give her. He felt like he had some sort of parental PTSD from raising Zoe on his own. In fact, his first therapist told him he had something similar.

The only nanny who had ever worked out was sitting beside him, and she had her own job now—one he doubted she would quit.

He felt like he was fighting an uphill battle raising Zoe, and he wasn't eager to reset that clock. The more he thought about it, the tenser he got.

"I did say never say never. But I can't promise anything."

Riley nodded, looking disappointed. Oliver wished he could promise he would ever feel ready for a second child, but he wasn't sure he would.

"I have time," she said, giving him a reassuring smile. "And I'm not saying I'm ready either, but we should be on the same page before we . . . take anything further."

He blinked. Did she know something?

She let it go after that, and soon both of them were distracted by Zoe introducing them to a little boy she was proclaiming her new best friend, which led to a conversation with the boy's parents while their kids played.

But Oliver kept circling back. He felt so sure about not wanting more kids, but worried that him not wanting them would give Riley a reason to say no.

She seemed to be lost in thought for parts of dinner, but she wasn't in bad spirits. He kept watching her, waiting for her to further argue her desire for kids. Most people would, but she gave him the space he needed.

He laid awake later than she did that night, feeling like he was somehow in the wrong. He didn't ever think about doing it all again, because his days before Riley were only trying to survive one moment to the next.

But if Riley wanted to . . . then maybe he could. He tried to imagine her with a baby, and God, she would look gorgeous holding one. He could see her smiling down at them, all of her joy in her gaze.

But then he remembered the sound of Zoe's endless screams, and the vision shattered.

He didn't want to put her through the stress of having a baby, but he almost couldn't say no, because he could imagine her full, bright smile. He knew once he saw that, he could never turn her down.

She wasn't even arguing with him about it. She didn't push him to change his mind or meet her in the middle. He knew she would never do that, and it was one of the things that made her so kind to others. It was what made her a great mother, even.

He rolled over to gaze at her sleeping face. This was the one thing they disagreed on, but knowing she would be by his side throughout anything made him want to say yes.

Chapter Ten

Riley

Since Zoe's adoption, Jane had gotten into the habit of asking Riley to bring her over for the night every few weeks. Zoe and Jane got along far better that Jane and Riley ever had.

She had gotten a lot of time with her grandmother with Riley's and Oliver's busy schedules. Since Jane could work from home more than either of them could, it worked out. Ever since Oliver's job had *finally* slowed down a few weeks ago, Zoe had been with them more often than not.

But her mother always wanted to see Zoe, so after three weeks, she'd called to ask if she could stay the night.

Riley, of course, had said yes.

When Riley walked into her mother's house, she expected to say hi and get Zoe settled in.

The last thing she was prepared for was for Jane to whisk Oliver away.

"Huh," Riley said, looking at Zoe. "Guess she needed to talk to your dad."

"Is there ice cream?" Zoe asked.

"You know what? I bet there is. I'll help you get some."

Normally, Riley wouldn't have agreed to ice cream in the afternoon because it made her ridiculously hyper, but her mother hadn't even said hello, so this was payback.

After getting Zoe settled with two scoops of cookies and cream ice cream with extra chocolate sauce on top, Riley sat on the couch and waited. The moment Oliver and Jane came from around the corner, she asked, "Are you done conspiring against me?"

"Oh, Riley," Jane said, rolling her eyes. "We were talking about something to do with my work. Nothing to worry about."

He nodded, but she didn't believe either of them. She wondered if Oliver had mentioned his possible plans to propose to Jane. If so, her mother would run with it.

Maybe Riley would finally get the family ring she'd wanted forever, but she doubted Jane would even give it to her considering it was such a treasured heirloom.

"How are things going?" Jane asked. She noted the change in conversation.

"Things are fine," she replied.

"I'm finally done with the crisis at work," Oliver added. "This is a perfect time for you to watch Zoe, actually. I haven't had time with Riley in forever."

"You two need time together. Especially for *exciting* things."

Wow. Her mom was laying it on *thick*.

"I gave her ice cream," Riley pointed out. "I probably wouldn't have if you had said hello."

Her mother laughed. "Zoe at her worst is only half as bad as Luke and Landon at their best. I'll be fine."

She remembered when Jane said only good things about Amanda's kids. But then again, maybe she only remembered the good things.

Nowadays, her mother was putting in an effort to treat them both equally. Her reasons for seeing Riley as problematic laid with her and not Riley herself.

Riley was still working out how to acknowledge that what her mother did was shitty and also accept that it was good she was trying.

It was a tough balancing act.

"Then I guess we'll head out." Riley stood and hugged her mother and Zoe before leaving.

"Does your mom know about therapy?" Oliver asked when they climbed into the car.

"No," she said, "but I'm used to not telling her the details of my life. She never really wanted to hear them. Plus, I don't know how she'd react."

"Why?"

"It was never seen as something we needed. Therapy was for the really fucked-up kids—the ones going through actual hell. My mom always said we weren't in a bad enough position for that."

"Do you think she'd say that now?"

She shrugged. "Honestly, I don't know if I want to find out."

"I suppose that's fair, but maybe consider telling her when you're ready. She seems open to change. Maybe she'd take it better than you think."

"Maybe," she admitted. "I might talk to her about it when we pick up Zoe."

"In your own time," Oliver said. "You're doing really well with this therapy thing, though. I can see a difference."

"I can too," she said honestly. "I'm so glad Camilla suggested it. I need to tell her thank you the next time I see her."

Oliver pulled onto the highway. Riley frowned, knowing it wasn't the way to the house.

"Where are we going?" she asked.

"Dinner. It's been too long since we had any time to ourselves. How about Alexander's?"

"I could be up for that. They have a tiramisu that I would die for, but it's *so* expensive."

"I think I can afford it," Oliver said with a wink.

Riley blushed and fought the urge to tell him she could pay.

"That would be nice, thank you." The words felt odd on her tongue; Oliver's bright smile told her she'd done the right thing.

Alexander's was busy, but thankfully it wasn't too long of a wait. They walked to the back of the restaurant, and Riley felt almost giddy to be on a date.

They hadn't had a typical relationship progression. Sometimes it was nice for it to be the two of them in a nice restaurant alone.

Over dinner, they discussed, of all things, stocks, but since both of them worked in business, it was interesting to compare what Riley did every day to what Oliver did.

After dinner, he took her to the local planetarium where they finished a romantic late-night date. It was a beautiful show where they learned about their place in the solar system.

Riley could have cried at the realization of how small they were in the universe. It was one of the shows she never would have taken herself to, but Oliver had picked it out for her and somehow, it was perfect.

At the end of it, she half expected him to pull out a ring or something, but when the show was over, he was offering her his arm to hold onto and not a velvet-lined box.

She couldn't tell if she was relieved not to be proposed to in front of a bunch of strangers, or disappointed she wasn't engaged.

After the show, Oliver revealed he had booked a backstage event for them, where they got to meet the program educator and see the machinery up close. Riley could have talked to the employee for hours about space. She only understood about half of what was said, but she felt like she knew more than she ever had about the stars.

"I loved that," she said, looking up at the sky as they walked to the car. There was far too much light pollution to see anything, but she could remember what the simulated total darkness looked like.

"I'm glad," he said. He looped an arm around her shoulders and pulled her in for a kiss in the middle of the parking lot.

God, she loved kissing him. She'd never expected to be with such a perfect and caring man so soon after David left her, and she didn't regret one moment of it.

They didn't see eye to eye on kids, but they shared so much else. Maybe in a few years he would be ready. Maybe someone else she knew would have a baby and she would be able to cure her baby fever.

As much as she wanted kids of her own, she knew she loved Oliver more, and he and Zoe were enough.

While Oliver drove home, the decision cemented itself in Riley. She would be sad, but she would never push him into anything he wasn't comfortable with. She wasn't that type of person.

The house was quiet and clean when they returned. Riley tried to ask if he wanted to watch a movie, and but he kissed her before she could.

"Why don't we have a change of scenery for once?" he asked, his voice low.

All other thoughts left her brain as he pulled her to the couch. His lips were insistent on hers. His cedar scent enveloped her, and she couldn't resist the thrill that shot up her spine at doing this in the living room for once.

Eventually, his hand cupped her breast, sending shockwaves across her body. She moved his fingers so they could slip under her shirt, and he could touch the skin directly. His slow, teasing motions made her shiver, and soon she couldn't take it. She straddled him, pressing against his hardness to feel more of him. She moved up and down his length, treating herself to the pressure she needed.

She knew she could easily cum from this alone, but she wanted it to be with no layers between them. Slowly, she removed his shirt, and he did the same with hers. She caught his intense eyes, trained only on her, and her body shivered with the expectation of what was going to come next.

They didn't even make it to the bedroom. The remaining clothes came off in only a few moments, and she felt him press against her entrance. She was so lost in the experience that he almost forgot to do one thing.

"Wait," she said, and he stilled. His cock pressed insistently against her entrance, but he didn't move. "I've been terrible about taking my birth control."

"You want me to use a condom?"

"Yes," she said. "Sorry."

He kissed her forehead. "It's not a problem. I think I have some in our room."

She moved off of him and watched as he went to the bedroom. The interruption did nothing to impede her libido, and by the time he was back, she was kissing him again.

He paused to roll on the condom but wasted no time lining himself up with her entrance. She moaned as he slowly pushed into her, stretching her in the way she liked.

Oliver pressed the pad of his thumb against her clit as she moved, which made her body tighten with pleasure. She moved her hips up and down his length, letting his hand press against her with each movement.

She moaned as she rocked, feeling her core warm as pleasure overtook her. All other thoughts fell away as she lost herself in feeling. Her body rose to a climax and crashed down with a pleasurable wave.

"Fuck, Riley," he said under his breath, and he rolled them over until he was on top of her. "You have no idea what you do to me."

She didn't have it in her to answer. She was too busy still feeling the aftereffects of her orgasm, and when he slammed into her, her sensitive body readied for more.

"The way you feel when I'm in you," he muttered, kissing at her jaw as he relentlessly pushed inside. "One of the days I'm going to make you cum as many times as you can."

She couldn't imagine being selfish enough to take him up on that, but the words lit her nerve endings on fire.

Her body tightened as he fucked her, and she felt herself climbing another impossible peak. She wasn't even touching her clit, and while she'd never came this way before, she was powerless to stop it.

"I want to hear you," he forcefully whispered into her ear, and that was all it took. She came, her body crumbling apart as she gasped for air. She clenched her entire self, and she saw stars. His thrusts grew rougher and he came with her name on his lips in a stuttered cry.

As her mind returned to her, she could only think how *amazing* that orgasm was.

"Holy shit," Oliver said, out of breath.

"I think I died and went to heaven."

"You and me both."

Oliver

Riley was lying on his shoulder, her head a comforting weight. They relaxed in tired silence after what they'd just done, and he wondered if things could possibly get any better.

"Shit," she muttered and suddenly sat up.

"What?" Oliver asked, frowning.

"Nothing bad. I need to call my doctor tomorrow and see if they've received the birth control implant I'm switching to. I keep forgetting to."

He nodded. He was grateful Riley had stopped him and told him to use a condom, but it was always a hassle keeping them where Zoe couldn't find them.

"It's been a while since you had your first appointment. Did they delay it?"

"My insurance did. They thought I was still on my mom's policy, which actually dropped me last year when I turned twenty-six, so I had to give them the new insurance information and wait for that to get all squared away before they would even ship it." She shook her head and set a reminder on her phone. "There. That should fix it."

He welcomed her back into his arms, already missing her warmth. He found himself wishing, not for the first time, that he could take away any and all burdens for her.

But unfortunately, he couldn't add her to his admittedly very good insurance until she was married to him. And beyond that, he couldn't fix everything for her.

He sighed. Maybe he should have proposed tonight, but he didn't want to pop the question without knowing for sure she'd say yes.

Plus, he also wanted their family and friends there.

"What?" she asked.

"Nothing," he replied. "I can see why you're stressed."

"This is nothing. I used to do more when I literally ran David's life." She rolled her eyes.

"You did everything?"

"Unfortunately. The man was so disorganized. Thank you for being able to do the basics of life by yourself."

"David is an idiot."

"Enough about him. I'm glad we finally have some alone time. I was about to come to your job and strangle that asshole COO myself."

"That would be a sight to see." He chuckled. "He's pissed that we couldn't win the case, but between you and me, I wasn't that into defending us against his policies."

"For real," she said. "Has Sophie done anything else?"

Her back only tensed slightly, and Oliver had to admire how far she had come.

"It's been fine. After what you said in front of the office manager, she's been ignoring me."

Riley barked out a laugh.

"She was pissed the day you did it. I believe she tried to say you were the one after my money."

"Whatever. It's not the first time I've heard that."

He rolled his eyes. "I'm sorry you even have to deal with this. Hopefully with therapy you're adjusting to everything."

"It's okay. I have you through it all."

Oliver kissed her, relieved that therapy was helping her clear all the hurdles in life he couldn't help her jump over himself. Her shoulders didn't tense as much these days and he could see her full smile again.

She yawned suddenly, the sound of it catching Oliver by surprise. "Okay, I'm suddenly *exhausted.*"

"It's been a long night."

"Would you be offended if I went to sleep?"

"No," he said. "Never. Maybe I'll join you."

She smiled and rested her head on his shoulder. He watched her for a moment and was more than a little shocked when she drifted off immediately.

As she slept, he made a mental list of everything that had changed. Maybe she was tired from taking on so much responsibility with Zoe while he was dealing with the lawsuit—but that had been weeks ago. She'd gone off her birth control. Could that cause tiredness?

He let her sleep and went out into the living room to be sure the house was locked up. A worry that something was off nagged at him, like he was missing something important.

But when he came up empty, he dropped it and decided to go to bed.

Chapter Eleven

Riley

The next day, they arrived at Jane's house late in the afternoon, and let themselves into the house when a knock at the door went unanswered.

Zoe was still in her pajamas, eating popcorn and watching a movie. She was happily entertained, but still gave Oliver and Riley a huge hug.

"Have fun?" Riley asked.

"Yes! We watched *Moana*, *Sleeping Beauty*, and *Frozen*!"

"But you hate *Frozen*," Riley reminded. That was one of the first things Zoe ever said to her.

"I like Elsa . . ."

"As long as you had fun," Oliver said, ruffling her hair.

Jane came around the corner and startled a little at their presence.

"Oh, you two are here!" Jane said. "How about you stay for dinner? Amanda and the boys are coming."

While she was still hurt at Amanda's comment weeks prior, Riley was beginning to move past it. Amanda had been polite when they'd run into each other at Oliver's office, so maybe dinner would go well.

"I don't think we have dinner plans," she replied, glancing at Oliver for confirmation.

He shook his head, seeming to be fine with staying.

Zoe was excited to stay in her pajamas. She went back to watching her movie and eating popcorn. Riley and Oliver got drafted to help with dinner. Jane was a powerhouse in the kitchen. She was a great cook but wanted everything a certain way.

Last Christmas, Riley had told Oliver not to question anything, and go along with whatever her mother said. He stuck to that advice even now.

Amanda, Luke, and Landon arrived at five. Amanda was still in her work outfit, looking dressed up. Riley was in a floral shirt and cardigan. She looked a little nicer than usual, but that was only because most of her flannels were dirty.

For a moment, she felt inferior, then she reminded herself she had no reason to. She wasn't worth any less than her sister.

Amanda's curly hair was a touch messier than it used to be, and she had dark rims under her eyes. She'd looked like this ever since the divorce was announced.

"Hey, mom," Amanda said tiredly, pulling Jane into a tight hug. She saw Riley and Oliver and she perked up. "I thought you guys might be here."

"Zoe seemed content to stay," Oliver said. "So, we figured it wouldn't hurt."

Amanda smiled at Oliver, and Riley felt a stronger-than-usual flush of possessiveness. The same had happened at the office. Riley had meant to talk to Sally about it, but there always seemed to be more pressing issues to deal with before they ran out of time.

Riley felt an unusual swell of emotion, but she pushed it down, knowing she could deal with it later when she was alone.

But it burned in her chest, stronger than normal. She hoped it would stay under control until the end of their dinner.

"Hey, how have you been?" Riley asked, hugging her sister.

"Oh, you know. Terrible as usual." Amanda's lips thinned. "James is doing God knows what while I raise our kids."

"I'm sorry. You deserve better."

"Yeah," she said, and then turned to Oliver. "It's nice to see you out of the office. You've basically been living there."

"It's good to be out of the office."

"What he was there for finally died down. It's been nice having him back by five every day," Riley added.

They were momentarily interrupted by Jane calling for Oliver's assistance. Once he was gone, Riley battled with the feeling of pure *relief* that he wasn't in the same room as Amanda, and then kicked herself for even being worried about it.

Everything was *fine*. It was only one comment.

"Wow," Amanda said, sounding a little distant, "even before you guys were dating he barely ever left that early."

"He's making up for lost time."

"Lucky," she said, her voice low.

Maybe Riley shouldn't have mentioned the extra time with him in order to spare Amanda's feelings, but she could imagine Sally's shake of her head.

No. Amanda's feelings weren't her responsibility. Just as she didn't want to step in and force Amanda and Oliver apart based on her own feelings.

"I could tell it's taking a toll on her," Oliver said, walking over. He placed a warm hand on her back.

"Yeah," Riley said, sighing. She never told Oliver what Amanda had said a while ago, and she was glad she hadn't. This would have been horribly awkward.

Jane asked for help with setting the table. Oliver offered to do that while Riley made sure the kids were ready for dinner. When they all sat down, Jane brought out a delicious-smelling casserole.

The kids tore into that first. Riley eyed them, wondering if they would pick up on the finely grated vegetables she and Jane had added.

"So," Amanda started. Riley noticed she had a mug instead of a regular glass, which was usually when she was drinking wine and didn't want Riley to see. "Any big news?"

Jane glanced at Oliver of all people, but he looked . . . not quite bewildered, but also not calm.

Riley bet it had to do with the proposal.

"The newly opened shop was featured in the *Nashville Scene*," Riley said.

"Really?" Jane asked. "Was it a good review?"

"Thankfully, yes. But it's all Camilla's coffee. It's none of my doing."

"You come up with amazing marketing tactics to get people in there," Oliver added, shaking his head. "You deserve a lot of the credit."

She blushed at the praise. She tried not to brag about her job, because she was still a barista most of the time. She just happened to be one of the few with full health coverage and a salary that was more than livable.

"Maybe," Riley said. "I'm glad it's working out well. Camilla and I have a revenue sharing thing going on. I got my first payout a few weeks ago."

And it had been more than expected. Riley suspected Camilla had shared more than agreed upon. When she tried to tell her, Camilla stated she was too bad at math to notice or fix it, and ran off.

"On top of your salary?" Amanda asked. "Man, maybe I should have worked in coffee brewing."

"Customers can be awful. I don't think you would like it."

"I don't know," Amanda said. "I think Oliver can agree work has been awful since Richard took over."

"Don't even mention him to me." Oliver rolled his eyes. "I can't tell you much, but I *can* say all of those emails did not come from us."

"I didn't think so. You and Jack actually care about your employees. I don't know why the guy was even hired in the first place."

"Investors," he replied. "They control more than everyone realizes."

"Well, maybe they'll learn. I hear the woman who lost her breaks is getting a good payout."

"I can't talk specifics . . ." Oliver said, but he nodded the confirmation anyway.

Amanda laughed. Riley felt a pit grow in her stomach and she forced herself to stifle an out-loud groan. There was no reason for her to be like this. Oliver *wasn't* interested in Amanda. He never was. Her comment hadn't even been brought up again, and she had no definitive proof that Amanda was even thinking about Oliver in that way ever since she said it.

This wasn't real. This was her abandonment issues coming out at a bad time.

"Honestly, you should just do both roles," Amanda said. "I think you'd be good at them."

"Maybe I'll get a promotion and get double pay."

"Oh, that would be *so* many toys for Zoe. As if she's not spoiled enough."

Riley gritted her teeth, resisting the urge to interject. This wasn't what she thought it was. She was overreacting.

"Yeah, like she needs more things . . . but I'm sure she will ask for them."

"They always do. God, I wished we talked like this when I was still your assistant."

"Well, you know how I like to keep it at work."

"Yes, but if we had talked, maybe it would be *us* together."

There was a sound of a fork hitting a plate, and Riley realized it was hers.

Breaths coming out heavily, she wanted to blow up. This was how fights went with Amanda. She would say something mean, Riley would stand up for herself, and then Jane would take Amanda's side because Riley was the one who caused a scene.

A small hand grabbed hers.

Zoe.

The little girl looked at her with wide eyes. Riley wasn't sure how much Zoe understood, but she could guess she saw how hurt her mother was.

She grounded herself with the feeling of Zoe's hand in hers. She knew she needed to defend herself.

She could say how wrong it was for Amanda to say something like that not only in front of Oliver, but in front of the kids. She could say jealousy wasn't a good look on Amanda, that she needed to grow up instead of making inappropriate comments at the dinner table.

But then Riley could hear her mother's defense of what Amanda had said.

It wasn't that bad, Riley. You're overreacting. What she's saying is true.

And at those imagined words, her fight left her. The hurt of her sister's comments hit her before she could open her mouth, and now she was near tears at the dinner table.

God, what if they all secretly agreed?

She almost wished she could've stayed angry. Instead, shame prickled her cheeks and wet her eyes. Burning heat surged through her face, and she couldn't take it.

She'd always been a fighter, but this was a new level of pain—one she couldn't turn into words. Everyone's eyes on her were too much.

The last thing she wanted was to leave, but she didn't feel like she had a choice. She couldn't take being in the same room as all of this.

"Excuse me," she said, her voice cracking. She stood, gently pulling her hand out of Zoe's. She power walked to the kitchen where she could be alone. The first thing she saw was a wine bottle on the counter.

She glared at it, and for a dangerous, traitorous moment, she thought about drinking it, but it only sent a flash of rage down her spine.

It seemed she still had a little bit of fight left in her.

She remembered the mug Amanda had used; Jane only had water.

As she poured the wine down the sink, she repressed the urge to hurl it at Amanda's head. She was the only one who dared to drink in her presence anymore.

Hurt bubbled into anger, and Riley's entire body tightened.

Amanda *knew* she struggled with drinking. Why couldn't she wait until she was home to go for the wine?

Her cheeks were wet and her throat ached. As the last drops of the wine poured down the drain, she could feel her will failing her. One sob escaped her, and then two more. Before she knew it, she'd slid onto the floor, crying and alone as her feelings overtook her.

Oliver

For a moment, there was only silence. Zoe watched Riley go with wide, worried eyes. Oliver glared over at Amanda, jaw clenched tightly.

"Wow. What's her deal?" She broke the silence as she rolled her eyes.

"Are you kidding me?" Oliver snapped.

Amanda turned to him with her mouth ajar.

"Amanda," Jane hissed out.

"What?" she asked. "It's just an observation."

"That was beyond disrespectful." Jane's voice was low, slow, but serious.

"What's going on?" Luke asked. "Why is Aunt Riley upset?"

Oliver glanced at the kids. "Go play in the other room, please."

"But this is—" Landon began.

"I'll take them," Zoe said, grabbing her cousins. Oliver didn't use this tone with kids very often. Zoe knew he meant business.

And he would explain it to her later.

Jane threw her napkin on the table. "You have no idea if that is true."

"Why is this such a big deal? She wasn't offended the first time I said it."

"You've said it before?" Oliver asked.

"Yes, when she was helping me clean the house."

He remembered that day. Riley was distant and nervous. He'd thought she was just in a bad mood from seeing Amanda, but he had no idea her sister had said something so *wrong*.

He couldn't imagine what Riley was thinking.

"It doesn't matter *what* you've said before or how it was taken," Jane cut in. "You do *not* make comments about your sister's relationship. You are to respect Riley and her life choices."

"I don't disrespect them, but you have to admit she's a little out of her league. I mean, look at him and look at her."

"And what does that mean? Explain that to me."

Amanda blinked. "Explain what?"

"Explain why we are mismatched. In detail. Because I'm struggling to understand."

"I-I mean, she's *Riley*. She's always been the girl who doesn't care about hair or makeup. She wears gross, old flannels. You're not like her *at all*."

"And who are you to decide we don't match? She's Riley and that's all I need. You don't get to question it. And even if you did, you should be keeping your opinions to yourself."

"But why her? God, you looked like you *hated* her the day after you met her. What the hell happened?"

"I fucking fell in love with her, that's what." The expletive rushed out of his mouth, and he was glad the kids weren't around to hear it. "But if I need to explain exactly how, then I can answer that too." He paused a moment to take a deep breath. "Let's start with her selflessness with how she *adopted* Zoe the moment she could. Or we could talk about how her smile could light up a city with no power. How about we bring up her incredible sense of humor. Or maybe the fact that she is always herself without caring what *anyone* thinks, despite your best efforts to make her insecure her entire life."

He stood, throwing his napkin on the table beside Jane's. He needed to get to Riley, but he wasn't done.

"All she ever needed to be was herself. I love *her*, and I will tell her every bit of this after she walks down the aisle and marries me. The timing of your divorce doesn't matter because I would have chosen her on a dark night with my eyes shut. You could have been single. You could have been pursuing me for years. But the moment she walked through the door, I was hers, and it will *never* change."

His chest heaved. His heart raced. He knew Riley was upset and he needed to take care of her. Amanda didn't deserve any more of his time.

"Jane, can you keep the kids busy while I go make sure Riley is okay?"

"O-of course." Jane's voice shook, and she stared at him like he was someone she didn't recognize. Both she and Amanda did, but he didn't care. Every word he said was true.

What he found in the kitchen almost broke him. Riley was alone, curled into a ball on the floor. She was sobbing silently, her shoulders shaking with the weight of what was said.

He knew her history. He knew her fears. This should have *never* been said to her.

"Riley," he said, kneeling next to her.

"No," she said, her voice thick. "You need to be with Zoe. Not watching me have a fucking meltdown on 1990s linoleum flooring."

"They're okay. They're in the other room."

Riley didn't answer him.

"Hey, I'm . . . I—" Oliver couldn't find the words to say. He knew Amanda was her sister, but he couldn't help that the other woman wasn't acting like it. "She's a bitch."

Riley looked at him, shocked. "What did you say?"

"Amanda's a bitch. Well, she's acting like one, anyway."

"I-I'm sorry. Did you just say *bitch*?"

"I think this calls for it."

Riley's face fell again, and she nodded. "Yeah, maybe."

"You've heard what Amanda said before."

She didn't look at him. Her eyes were on her hands, which twisted in her lap. "Yeah, I did."

"Why didn't you tell me?"

"Because I . . . I was worried you'd think she was right, and it would be the catalyst of you choosing *her*. And now I'm crying and looking so stupid for getting all upset about this. It wasn't even that big of a deal."

He blinked, unable to process seeing her reaction to being insulted in such a way by her own sister. She was taking it all in as if it were *her* fault, and that was the furthest thing from the truth.

It was one thing to know his partner felt such pain. It was another to see it.

"I'm sorry," she muttered.

"No," he said. "This isn't your fault. Amanda disrespected your relationship, she—"

"But is she wrong?" she asked. "Everyone says we don't fit. Even I don't know why the fuck you chose me—"

"Riley, don't."

"It's a fair question," she said, finally looking him in the eyes. "You could have anyone in the world."

"But I want you."

She shook her head. "I don't understand why."

"Because you were the missing piece of the puzzle. I've dated women that were magazine-page perfection and that did nothing for me. I don't need another shallow girlfriend. I need *you*, the woman who helps loosen me up, who gives me a reason to smile every day. I never wanted someone to keep me in a box. I need someone to get me out of it. And that's you."

"And what happens when I've gotten you out of your box? Then will you be done with me?"

"No, because I broke out of it to be with *you*. And I'd do it all again just to see you smile."

Her eyes met his, and instead of the fear, he saw shock. Before he knew it, she had her arms wrapped around his neck and was pulling him close. His hands settled on her back instinctively.

"I know you have a hard time believing it, but you are one of the most beautiful women I've ever seen. I saw it the first time you smiled in my direction, and I still see it to this day. Anything you see as an imperfection is perfect to me because it's *you*, Riley. This is how love is. I know you know that because you do it for me and Zoe."

"You guys *are* perfect."

"No, we're not, but you still love us anyway. Why can't I do the same?"

She was silent, and he was tempted to pull away to study her face, but the lure of her body against his kept him from moving.

"Thank you," she said, her voice shaky.

"You deserve this and more."

"I'm working on believing it."

He pressed a long kiss to her forehead, thankful she had listened, but hating every single person who made her question who she was.

"I love you, and I would never have chosen anyone else. I can only prove it by standing by your side. But trust me when I say it's the easiest thing I'll ever do."

She was quiet, but her arms tightened around him.

Oliver didn't care how long she wanted to sit here with him. He would be there for as long as she needed him.

After a few minutes, she pulled away, wincing. "Okay, I need to get up. Sitting on the floor fucking hurts."

He felt the tension in his chest release when he saw that her tears had dried and she was looking like herself again.

"I guess we need to go face the music," she muttered. "I hope I didn't piss off my mom by storming in here."

"Jane was too busy being furious at Amanda for that."

She frowned. "She was mad at her and not me?"

"No one is mad at you. Well, Amanda might be, but she was in the wrong."

"That's a first."

"I hate that it is, but I'm glad I didn't have to bite *both* of their heads off."

"That I'd like to see," she said. He pulled himself up off the floor and helped her to her feet.

Riley tightly held his hand as they left the kitchen. Her eyes darted around the room, as if she was going to get in trouble for something that wasn't her fault in the first place.

"Riley," Jane said, standing from the dinner table. "Are you okay?"

"No," she said, "but I will be."

Jane sighed and walked over to give her a hug. "I'm sorry, sweetie."

Riley's eyes widened, but she gained her composure quickly. "It's okay."

"No, it isn't," Jane insisted, pulling away. "I got lucky with you. Despite my poor parenting, you turned out to be such a kind person. I wish the same were true for Amanda."

Riley blinked, a few tears falling down her cheeks. He could see the impact of Jane's words.

"Where is she?" Riley asked, voice breaking.

"She's sulking in her room."

Riley glanced in the direction of the stairs, almost like she wanted to go find Amanda herself, but Oliver was grateful when she didn't.

"Thank you," she said quietly, "for not blaming me."

"I said I wanted to be better, and I will be. My therapist is helping me with that."

Riley's eyes bulged. "Really?"

"Yes," Jane said. "Perhaps you should go see one too."

"I have been for a while."

"Good," Jane said, smiling. "You always were the one willing to do the difficult work. I'm proud of you."

"Thank you," she said, and he could tell by the crack in her voice that she meant it.

Chapter Twelve

Riley

There were some days Riley hated working in public.

It had been a few days since the disaster dinner at her mother's house, and Riley had been walking on eggshells ever since. Her emotions were out of whack, and she knew it was partly because of the strain between her and Amanda, and partly because she had officially stopped taking her birth control pills since Oliver was okay using a condom.

Mood swings were normal because of all of that, right?

She was going to bring it up in therapy, but her appointment was later in the week. Her goal was to keep herself under control until then.

The thing was, Riley wasn't angry and taking it out on her employees or customers.

No. It was that everything seemed to hit harder.

Luckily, her employees all gave her space. She already warned them she wasn't in the best place mentally, so she hoped they wouldn't lose all respect for her if she wound up sobbing in the stockroom over something random.

On this day, Riley did well keeping her cool through the morning rush, and things cleared up after nine. She had time to clean up the shop and make sure there were no dishes left on tables.

She thought maybe she would make it through her day without a crying episode, but then a family walked in.

She didn't usually have problems with families. They came in all the time since Camilla's shops had some of the best cinnamon rolls in town, but she spied a baby carrier and could feel the emotion coming on.

Since they had last talked, she hadn't put much thought into Oliver's position on kids. She figured she would be able to deal with it, especially since she had a full schedule and one child already. She knew that she wanted him more than she wanted kids.

There was nothing wrong with that. She didn't think people needed to have children if they didn't want to—but she always wanted them. Even when her life had been a dumpster fire, she always wistfully looked at families with tiny babies.

Riley wanted that experience for herself, but now she knew she wouldn't have it, unless she wanted to force one on Oliver.

But she would never do that. She just wished she had met him earlier.

The family walked to the register and placed their order. They wanted a lot of food, and the mom struggled to carry all of it to their table.

"I'll come back for it," her partner said.

"I've got it," Riley replied, plastering a smile on her face and pretending she was fine. She helped them carry the food to their table.

"Thank you," the mom said gratefully. "Sorry, I keep forgetting I have a couple less hands than usual." She turned the carrier around while one of their other kids grabbed at a pastry.

Riley's eyes were caught on the smallest baby she had ever seen.

They were probably six weeks old, but swaddled in ample blankets and clothing, they looked tiny.

"You have a beautiful baby," Riley said, her chest heavy.

"Thank you."

"I have an adopted daughter, so I wasn't there for . . . this part."

The mom smiled, her eyes tired. "It's rough, but I know I'll look back and remember it fondly."

Riley nodded, emotion hitting her like a truck. Fuck, she really wanted this. She wanted the tiredness and the sleepless nights. She wanted to hold a tiny baby and take care of it. She wanted to experience the hell of pregnancy, morning sickness and all.

Oh shit. She was going to cry.

She excused herself before she lost it in front of the customers. She went to her office, which is where she finally let the tears fall.

This wasn't like her. She didn't cry like this. Sure, babies were cute. And sure, she might be mourning *not* ever having a baby like that should she stay with Oliver, but it shouldn't be this bad. Right?

She finally collected herself and decided not to think about babies for a while. She needed time to process before she could accept that being with Oliver meant not having any more kids.

It wasn't a perfect solution, but she was in therapy for a reason. This is what she could talk about. Maybe there was some weirdly deep emotional thing going on that she could unpack.

Riley just had to make it until later in the week.

When she left her office, she hung around the espresso machines so she wouldn't face customers. But eventually, a regular that Riley knew well came in, brown eyes wide.

"Are you okay?" Lily Miller asked the moment she saw her.

Lily was famous, but the only reason Riley knew that was because of the media storm that occurred once she escaped from an abusive family situation and permanently settled in

Nashville with her husband. When Riley invited a writing group to meet at the shop, Lily showed up and had become a consistent customer ever since, and she and Riley had struck up a friendship over time.

Riley was probably one of the very few people who knew where she was, considering both Lily and her husband had completely changed their appearances to be sure they weren't caught.

"I'm fine," Riley said, smiling. "Nothing to worry about."

"I don't know. I used to see that expression when I looked in the mirror, and that's saying something."

"Tiny babies make me emotional."

Lily's face scrunched in confusion, but then she seemed to accept it. "Sometimes food makes me emotional, so I get it."

"Oh, I should probably eat," Riley muttered. "I forgot breakfast."

"You *do* look a little pale."

"Yeah," she said, grabbing a cinnamon roll. "Sorry for bugging you with my weird mood. I'm really fine."

"It's okay. I owe you one for starting the writing group, and because I'm pretty sure you know who I am and have never told."

Riley smiled. "I'm no snitch."

Lily laughed. "I'm grateful for that. Now go take a break. You need one."

She didn't need to be told twice. At Lily's instruction, she went to the back to eat. By the time she returned, she only felt a little better.

Oliver

Oliver didn't usually see Amanda at work anymore, which was something he was grateful for, considering their last meeting.

But this morning he came in late after taking Zoe to school. It was eight-thirty when he got there, and it didn't cross his mind that this was the same time Amanda arrived.

When she met him at the bank of elevators, he almost opted to take the twenty flights of stairs to avoid her, but then she turned and saw him, and he knew he would look the fool if he ran.

To her credit, her face flushed and her eyes darted down to her feet. Oliver could only imagine what Jane had said to her after they left.

What Amanda had blurted out still made him sick to think about.

"So, uh, how's the weather?" she asked awkwardly as they got in. He glanced at her with an irritated frown. Luckily, no one else joined them in the elevator. When it closed, she let out a long sigh. "Okay . . . I'm sorry about what I said at dinner the other night. I'm in my own head about the divorce and I keep wondering what I could have done differently to not go through this."

"What you said was inappropriate."

"I know. My mom said I acted like a spoiled brat who wanted her sister's Barbie, and she's right. What you and Riley have is special, and I'm sorry I was immature about it."

Well, at least she knew she was wrong.

"I'm not the only one you should apologize to," he reminded her.

"I know," she replied. "But Riley is never going to forgive me for this."

"Why not?"

"Because I wouldn't if I were in her shoes."

"I don't think you know your sister all that well."

"Why should she?" Amanda said. "I made a terrible comment on her relationship, twice, and made her cry, which as far as I know, only her cheating ex made her do."

"I'm pretty sure I did when I fired her. She didn't forgive me right away, and she never had to, but she did anyway. So many people, myself included, have done bad things to her. We're all in the wrong, and I wish none of us had ever hurt her. And through all the abuse, she's still kind."

"How does she stay so nice? I want to burn down the world over my ex-husband and I know it's not even half of what she's gone through."

"She found something that keeps her grounded, and she focuses on that."

Amanda frowned, then realization hit her. "Zoe."

"Yeah."

She nodded. "Maybe . . . maybe I should take Luke and Landon to the train show coming up. They'd love it."

"If they're what keeps you grounded, then you should."

"I feel like I'm losing my mind."

"Maybe you should see a therapist."

She looked shocked. "What? I don't need to see a—"

"You wouldn't be the only one in your family seeing someone," he said pointedly. "And it's helped them. You need to talk to someone instead of lashing out at Riley."

"But *no one* in my family goes to therapy. We ignore each other and then move on."

"And how has that worked out for you all?"

She looked away. The doors slid open.

"Well . . . it's expensive," she said, not moving to get out of the elevator.

"The health insurance here only has a $10 copay."

Amanda blinked. "Seriously?"

"We made a personalized plan to include it. It's the one thing I refused to let Richard change. Use it, Amanda. Before you lose your sister."

Oliver wasted no more time in getting out of there. He hoped Amanda took his advice, but he also hoped he didn't see her again for a good, long while.

When he arrived at his office, Jack was waiting, arms crossed and looking angry. This was the day they had planned to let Richard go, but there was no reason for Jack to look this way.

"Did I do something wrong?" Oliver asked.

"It's not you. Emergency meeting. Now."

He followed Jack. His father didn't get angry often, but when he did, it was serious. They walked into the conference room, where Richard, Sophie, and Steph were all glaring at one another.

He could tell this was not going to be a pleasant meeting. Oliver sat in one of the chairs and watched his father walk to the front of the room. Had Richard somehow found out about their efforts to remove him?

"I have been informed," Jack began, "by an employee that Sophie and Richard were caught having an intimate relationship on our property."

"What?" Oliver asked. An employee caught the secretary of the legal team and the COO in the office? The same day he was going to get fired?

Oh, this was almost too good to be true.

"During work hours," Jack hissed.

Sophie looked ashamed. Richard beamed.

"I don't see why this is a big deal," he said. "She consented."

"We're in the middle of a legal battle about employee ethics and you were with the woman working directly under you! Our company is under scrutiny, and now on top of this lawsuit, I have to ensure one of the employees signs an NDA."

Oliver knew he couldn't say much. He had slept with Riley while she worked for him, but she also hadn't been employed by the company.

"Tell us why you did this, Sophie," Steph said, frowning.

"I was offered . . . a promotion."

Oliver stared at her. She looked sheepish, but he couldn't tell if she was acting or if she actually felt bad for being a part of this. Then again, Richard should have never offered her a promotion in exchange for sex in the first place.

"Richard, you are fired," Steph announced.

"You can't do that."

"All investors signed off on it this morning." She handed him a tall stack of papers. "It's all in here."

"After all I've done for this company?" Richard was red in the face.

"You've ruined our reputation and cost us millions," Jack snapped. "The investors are as angry as we are, and we are considering taking legal action against *you* if you do not leave quietly."

Richard stood, his face contorted in rage. "I'll talk to them myself. There is no reason for you to let me go when I worked my ass off day in and day out to ensure we did not lose this case, and *you* chose to settle."

"Do we need to get security?" Steph asked. Oliver could respect her boldness. He bet she didn't like Richard just as much as him and his father.

Richard scoffed and stormed out, slamming the glass door behind him. Several employees turned to look as he headed toward the elevator.

"Oliver," Jack said, his voice only slightly calmer, "you are to temporarily take over the COO role, and I will assist with any responsibilities you can't manage."

Oliver nodded. He knew it would be more work, but he'd been managing it before Richard was hired, so he knew what to expect.

"Sophie, please go back to your desk."

Oliver knew they couldn't retaliate against her, not if they wanted to avoid another lawsuit, so her employment was safe.

Then she opened her mouth.

"You can't do this to him. He told me how hard he worked for you all."

"That doesn't change our decision," Jack said.

"Then I quit."

"You what?" Steph asked, eyebrows raised.

"Yes. Effective immediately, I quit. He won't be jobless for long and I know I'll find myself in a better position if I follow him. Good riddance to you all. I wish you nothing but the worst."

She stormed out of the meeting room, following in Richard's footsteps.

Oliver watched her leave, trying to conceal his smile. His father was angry, but this might have been the best possible situation he could have asked for. Sophie and Richard gone in one day? He was free.

Sure, he would have a mountain of work to do, but it would all be worth it.

"I'll go sign the resignation papers," Steph said, sighing. She walked out of the room, leaving Oliver alone with his father.

"We are never letting investors make a decision again," Jack said lowly. "Maybe we should go public."

"Well, one good thing came out of all of this," Oliver countered. "They do deserve each other."

Jack sighed. "You know we will have to find a replacement and do a lot of work to keep the company running, right?'

"Honestly, I don't even care. We managed before him. We can manage after him."

"At least there won't be any more lawsuits," his father muttered.

"I'm ready for some peace around here."

His day was amazing after that. He texted Riley that he would be home late before managing to get a lot of work done. He hated he would be at the office more but was happy he could rebuild the company, and build back everything Richard destroyed.

When he got home, Zoe was in bed, and Riley was asleep on the couch. Oliver smiled at her and kissed her on the forehead, which woke her up.

"Hey," she said, her voice thick with sleep. "You're home."

"I am. Sorry about staying late, but you'll be happy to know that someone got fired."

"Oh, Sophie. No, wait, maybe the COO."

"Richard got fired and then Sophie quit."

"Why did Sophie quit?"

"Because she was caught having sex at work and followed him in an act of love."

"Holy shit, they slept together?"

"Apparently so. They deserve each other."

Riley laughed. "They do! I hope they're miserable for the rest of time."

"How was your day?" he asked, sitting next to her.

Her smiled waned. "It was . . . fine."

"Are you still back and forth between feeling good and feeling terrible?"

"Yeah," Riley said. "I'm going to bring it up in therapy on Thursday. If not, then I'll talk to my OBGYN when I go to finally get my new birth control. I hope it's nothing." She yawned.

"Me too," he replied. "But I do have to be at the office more. Can you take Zoe to school tomorrow?"

"Yeah," she said, her forehead creasing. He hated having to ask. "I'll make it work."

Chapter Thirteen

Riley

Riley figured out very quickly that she should not have agreed to take Zoe to school. She needed to be at the coffee shop at seven to help with the pre-work rush, but Zoe's school didn't open until seven-thirty. Plus, Zoe was frustrated at the change in her usual routine.

It was not a pretty affair. Riley kept a lid on her frustration while Zoe was in the car, but the moment she'd dropped off her cranky and tired daughter, she'd felt tears of frustration brimming.

Then, work was a mess. They didn't get any of their usual prep work done because Riley was late, two people called out, and there were more customers than usual lining up through the door.

After four hours working, she hadn't stopped once.

She had a bad habit of not paying attention to her needs when she was busy. She knew this, and sometimes all she could do was gulp down coffee until she had a free moment to sit and eat. Some days, she could get away with sitting in her office and scarfing a breakfast sandwich.

This was not one of those days.

Her headache started after the third customer complained that their drink was wrong. All she had time to do was take sips from a hidden cup of coffee in the tiny moments she had to breathe.

By noon, she was snappy and tired and was counting down the seconds until the other manager came in to relieve her.

But then one of her cashier's drawers didn't balance, so she had to fix that. After that, there was an issue with a coffee machine, and then she needed to go to the bank to deposit the money they had earned that day.

By the time she returned, she was lightheaded.

That was when she should have stopped. Lightheadedness was something she never experienced. In hindsight, it would have been better for her to take a break and actually eat something, but there was more work to do.

She helped with the unusual rush until she had to leave to get Zoe.

By then, her headache was pounding like a drum behind her eyes. Luckily, Zoe seemed to be content to talk about her own day. Apparently, she'd made a new friend and wanted to ramble all about it.

Which was fine, considering Riley could barely think of anything to say.

Oliver arrived home at seven, which wasn't as late as she expected. But in the four hours since Riley had been at the house, the shop had called her three times to ask questions.

She was beginning to feel sick, so sick that she couldn't even think about food. She was no doubt starving since she hadn't eaten anything all day, but the mere thought turned her stomach.

Instead of getting something to eat, she laid on the couch, which was where Oliver found her.

"Hey," he greeted.

Riley didn't answer.

"Are you okay?" he asked, and she heard him shuffle closer.

"Bad day," Riley muttered.

"What happened?"

Riley could only answer in a long, pained groan.

"You look pale," he said, pulling her hands off of her eyes.

"I *feel* pale."

"Have you eaten?"

"No."

"Let's start there. Let's go out. We can get whatever you want."

"I don't even know what I want."

"Okay, how about burgers?"

"Sounds gross."

"Pizza?"

A groan.

"Ice cream?"

"We need Zoe to eat real food first."

"Hm . . . Mexican?"

Riley paused. That was the only option that didn't make her want to throw up. "Okay, maybe that."

"Come on. I'll drive."

Riley nodded and slowly peeled herself off the couch.

That was her first mistake.

Her body was depleted.

No, it was past depleted.

The fumes she had been operating on vanished, and she had nothing left.

When she stood, clouds danced in her vision, and she grabbed onto the armrest for support. It didn't help.

Her world went black, and the last thing she saw was Oliver's panicked face.

Oliver

Oliver didn't like hospitals. He didn't have good memories of them.

When he was young, almost too young, a hospital was where he found out his mother wasn't coming home. In another hospital, many years later, he saw Zoe's mother physically turned away from their child, refusing to look at her daughter.

And now, he hated them even more because Riley needed one.

Oliver had called Jack while the ambulance was on the way. If there was one thing about his father he loved, it was that he was there in a crisis.

Zoe hadn't seen it happen, but she knew something was wrong. Oliver wasn't able to explain it to her because he was focused on making sure Riley was breathing, and didn't quite understand what had happened himself. Once Jack was there, he was able to answer Zoe's questions.

Jack was used to explaining hard things to kids. When Zoe tearfully asked what was going on, he gave accurate but simple answers.

Oliver wouldn't have trusted anyone else with this.

His drive to the hospital had his mind full of possibilities of what could have happened. Maybe her blood sugar tanked. She said she hadn't eaten. Maybe it was stress.

Maybe it was something more serious.

Riley didn't tell anyone when she was feeling bad. If she was busy, he knew she tended to run herself into the ground, but she'd been more tired, more emotional than usual.

He should have pushed her harder to go to the doctor. He should have offered to take her himself if she needed it.

Both of them had prioritized work, and Zoe, but in moments like these, he couldn't remember why. He should have made sure she was okay. She mattered so much more.

He didn't remember much about his childhood, but he remembered a pale face like Riley's on his mother in her final weeks, and *fuck*, there was no way he could stomach that. He'd spend all his money to cure her of anything like that.

When he pulled into the parking lot of the hospital, his hands were shaking and his mind was filled with a dozen possibilities, but he needed to be sure she was okay first.

He walked straight to the front desk and told the receptionist who he was here for.

"Are you related to her?" she asked, raising an eyebrow.

"I'm her . . . boyfriend."

"If I don't have a release form then I can't tell you much." She gave him an apologetic grimace. "If she wakes up, a nurse can ask if she wants you to know anything."

Oliver nodded numbly. He didn't like the usage of the word *if* on anything to do with her. He sat in the waiting room, knowing he needed to let Jane and Amanda know what was happening.

But his hands continued to shake and his heart raced. He couldn't do it.

He was normally great in a crisis. He had to be since he was a parent.

But this was Riley. All he could think about were the things he never said to her, how he never told her he wanted to marry her, how he didn't get to express his love for her in the right ways, and how he would do anything to see her again. He tried and failed to keep himself calm, but his brain was alight with possible things that could have happened to her.

Time passed, though he couldn't tell how much went by. All he could think about was her.

His body stiffened when he heard someone call out, "Mr. Brian?"

He jumped from the chair immediately.

"Ms. Emerson's awake, and she wants to see you."

Chapter Fourteen

Riley

Riley did not recommend passing out.

Her head was killing her, and she would kill for a glass of water. She could hear the beeping of a hospital monitor and felt an IV in her arm.

Yep, this sucked.

"Back with us?" the nurse asked.

"Unfortunately," Riley mumbled.

"We've set you up with an IV with some nutrients. A doctor will be in soon to talk to you."

"I guess it's not good news then."

The nurse gave her a wry smile. "You should definitely eat more, that's for sure."

Her face heated. If she passed out and ended up in the hospital because she forgot to eat, she would die of embarrassment.

And medical bills.

"Is my boyfriend here?"

"What's his name?"

"Oliver Brian."

"I'll see. You'll have to sign a release form."

She nodded. She didn't want to be alone, though she assumed Oliver was probably *pissed*.

He walked in moments later, looking pale, shaken, and worried. For the first time, she realized how serious this must have looked from the outside.

"I'm fine," she said immediately.

"You are not fine." He used a voice normally reserved for Zoe when he wanted her to listen.

God, why did she forget to eat? Why didn't she just grab a pastry or anything while she was at work?

She looked at her hands, unable to say anything else. She had caused far too much worry in one day. She wanted to melt into the floor.

Oliver moved toward her, and Riley wondered if he was going to sit down and give her the lecture of her life, but then she was suddenly enveloped in the tightest hug she had ever been a part of.

"I'm . . . I'm sure it's nothing serious."

"Nothing serious?" he asked, pulling away. "You blacked out. What if it's . . . what my mom had?"

She hadn't thought of that, but she shook her head. "This doesn't feel like anything serious. I don't feel like something's wrong. I feel like I've run a marathon every day and haven't caught up."

"And that's not serious?"

"Yes, it's serious. But I can't afford to go to a bunch of doctors to tell me I just need to remember to eat. That's what they'll tell me here; the nurse already has. I can guarantee that's the final diagnosis."

"Riley, if it comes to it, I will pay for whatever you need done."

"Oliver—"

"No," he said firmly. "Don't fight me on this. I just spent God knows how long out there wondering if you were going to die."

She felt herself deflate. "I'm sorry," she apologized genuinely.

"Don't be sorry, but I want them to run tests. I need to know if this really happened because you forgot to eat or if it's something more serious."

She wanted to fight him on it, but she knew it was a losing battle. He was scared, and he had a valid reason to be. She didn't want to think about how he must have felt seeing her lose consciousness without any clue of what was going on. If she had been in his shoes, she would have done the same.

"Okay," Riley said. "They said the doctor was going to come talk to me. I'll . . . I'll mention the other stuff and see if they have tests they can run here. If not, I'll go to my usual doctor as soon as I'm discharged."

Some of the tension melted out of Oliver's shoulders. "Thank you."

"Well, I hear someone's awake." The doctor opened the door with a knock. He was an older man with a file in his hand.

"Um, yeah," Riley said.

"Are you the significant other?" he asked Oliver.

"Yes," Oliver said.

"Are you okay with him hearing your medical information?"

"Yeah, I signed the form."

"I see that. I just wanted to check." He smiled. "So, it looks like your blood sugar dropped and you fainted."

"I thought it was that."

"Did you run any tests to see if there are any other deficiencies? If something else is off?" Oliver asked.

"We ran the usual tests," the doctor said. "Other than the low blood sugar, most of it was normal."

"Most?" Both Riley and Oliver asked at the same time.

"We can explain the fainting pretty easily. What other symptoms were you having?"

"Mood swings, tiredness, headaches," Riley said, "but mostly in the last two weeks. It wasn't too worrisome. Well, until now."

The doctor nodded. "Well, then the answer is pretty simple. You're pregnant."

Silence.

"Excuse me?" Riley blurted out after a long, drawn-out moment. She racked her brain for an explanation, but none came. They had been safe the last time they said sex. Was there a time when they weren't?

It hit her then.

The shower. They hadn't used protection in the shower.

Shit. Riley had *known* that. She had meant to go get a Plan B pill, but she was so distracted with Oliver's possible proposal that she completely forgot about the task at hand.

That had been almost two months ago.

"We don't know how far along you are," the doctor said. "But your HCG levels are pretty high. When was your last period?"

"I don't know," she said dimly. "A while ago."

"Do you drink or smoke?"

Riley shook her head.

"Okay, that's good. I want to do an ultrasound to make sure everything looks good, but then you'll be free to go." The doctor smiled once more. "Any questions?"

"No."

The doctor looked between Oliver and Riley, gave a knowing nod, and walked out of the room without another word.

The moment they were alone, Riley began to process the news.

Pregnant? After Oliver had clearly stated how he never wanted another child?

It took her a moment to gather the courage to glance over at him. Oliver was completely still, staring at the space the doctor had left.

She knew he was going to be angry. He didn't want this, and she didn't blame him. He'd said he had some sort of trauma after Zoe was born, and now Riley was pregnant?

Fuck.

The last thing she wanted was to have him stick around solely out of duty—to raise a child he never truly wanted.

She'd rather do it on her own than force him into this.

Her thoughts were broken by a nurse entering the room.

"Time for an ultrasound!" she announced, completely missing the vibe in the room.

"Yeah, right," Riley said, getting up to move. Her body did not like that.

"No, no," the nurse said. "We're wheeling you over there." Another nurse brought in a wheelchair, which was, in a word, awful. She had to move slowly, and Oliver was the one who helped her into it without being asked. Did he even want to touch her after this? Or was this obligation? "Well, what do you say? Ready to go see the baby?"

"As ready as I'll ever be."

"Are you the father?" the nurse asked Oliver. "Do you want to go?"

Riley thought maybe he would say no, and she wondered if she would even blame him for it.

"Yes. I'll go."

Riley didn't know what to think of his curt tone. But she didn't have much time to mull it over because the nurse was wheeling her down the hall, chatting the whole way there.

Riley wished she had known more of what to expect of an ultrasound this early in a pregnancy, because having a wand up insider her was something she would have preferred to prepare for.

Luckily it was only mildly uncomfortable, not painful, and she was able to manage it. Oliver sat next to her, face unreadable as an image came onto the screen.

There were a few things Riley would consider a life-changing moment. One of them was when she found out David was cheating on her. Another was when she found Zoe at the playground when no one else could. The biggest one, until this moment, was when Zoe asked if she could call her "mommy."

This one didn't diminish any of the rest, but it changed her nonetheless. All she saw was a tiny bean that looked a little like a gummy bear, but the idea that this was her child, just like Zoe, made her world shift again, moving to accommodate a second child she thought she would never have.

Her choice was made then. If Oliver didn't want to have another child, she would do it on her own. She wanted this, and as long as she could do it, she would find a way to keep this child, even if it meant losing him.

"Here's the heartbeat," the nurse said, and the *ba-boom* sound that filled the room would be forever ingrained in her memory.

The nurse took a few measurements before removing the wand, and then she said she was done.

"I'll take you back to your room now, and I'll show the doctor what I found. Congratulations!"

Riley nodded and smiled. She didn't dare look at Oliver because if he mentioned anything about not wanting this child, she was going to have to tell him she would never consider not having it, and then they would have to go their separate ways.

After she was back in her room, there was a tray of food waiting for her. It wasn't anything fancy—a slice of meatloaf, a pile of mashed potatoes and vegetables, and surprisingly, ice cream.

Riley tore into that first.

After she had eaten everything, her stomach was full but she only felt marginally better.

She had completely forgotten Oliver was in the room while she ate, and now he was staring at her. She had no clue what he was thinking, but maybe she didn't want to.

"I know this isn't what you wanted," she said. "So, you don't have to stay."

That got him to look at her. "What?"

"You told me you didn't want another kid, and I don't expect you to go back on that because of this. I can handle this myself."

"And what does that mean?" he asked harshly.

"It means you have an out."

"I don't *want* an out."

"You said you didn't want more kids. You don't have to have another one."

"So, you don't want the baby?"

"I never said I don't want the baby. *You* don't, Oliver. And I'm saying you can walk away now. We split Zoe and I raise this one on my own."

"You raise them?"

"Yes, me. And don't you dare give me any shit for it either. I want this kid, and if you don't, that's fine. I'm not going to hold you to anything you didn't plan for."

"And you planned for this?"

Riley frowned. Was he saying that she tried to get pregnant despite his wishes? Did he truly think she was that manipulative?

That was when the door burst open and Jane walked in.

"Of course my daughter wants to see me," Jane said, her voice tense. "And you can call as much security as you want, you will not stop me!"

"Mom?" Riley asked. "What are you doing here?"

"Oh, Riley!" Jane said, running over to the bed. A very annoyed-looking nurse walked in after her.

"Is it okay if she's here?" the nurse asked.

"Yeah," Riley said. "Mom, how did you know I was here?"

"Hospitals call next of kin when someone is hurt," Jane said. "Both Amanda and I were called."

"Oh, no. Please tell me Amanda did not just find out I was brought to the hospital because I forgot to eat."

"We don't know anything yet. I just got here."

Riley blushed. "I'm fine. There's nothing . . . seriously wrong with me."

Riley and Oliver exchanged a look. They were the only two who knew what was really going on, and she didn't know how much he would be willing to share with Jane.

She didn't find out because his phone rang. He looked irritated as he pulled it out, and she wondered if he was seriously about to accept a work call while she was still in the hospital.

"It's my dad," Oliver said. "He's watching Zoe, so I should take this."

"Was Zoe there?" her mom asked. "Is she okay?"

"Yes, she was there and . . . no, probably not. I'll step out into the hall to take the call."

Guilt washed over Riley. Shit, Zoe was probably freaking out.

"No, don't feel bad." Jane grabbed Riley's hand. "Sometimes these things happen, and kids are around. Remember when I had that stomach ulcer?"

She did remember, and it wasn't a fun day. But she never blamed her mother for it.

"I hate that this happened," Riley said. "I cannot believe I passed out because I didn't eat all day."

"It's okay," Jane replied. "But you need to get better about taking care of yourself. I know you're busy and you have a lot on your plate. You're so busy taking care of everyone else, you need to remember to take care of *you*."

"I know," she said, feeling lectured like a child, even though Jane's tone was compassionate. "And I've gone longer without eating. By the time I realized I'd done it, I was so nauseous I couldn't even think about it."

"You need one of those meal kits I saw on TV the other day. I think I have a coupon code somewhere."

"Yeah," Riley said. "You know what, I'll sign up for it."

Her mother looked shocked for a moment, but then smiled. "I'm glad you're listening."

"I think going to the ER for fainting is a good wake-up call."

That and being pregnant.

Riley groaned to herself. She still needed to figure out where Oliver stood on this.

Would she be doing this alone? Maybe.

Would she be angry? Definitely.

"I need to go," Oliver said, coming back into the room. "Zoe is inconsolable and I . . . Riley, I have to go."

"It's Zoe," she said. "I understand."

"I'll get her home," Jane added, smiling at him.

"They said they would be discharging her soon. I just . . . I'm sorry. I have to go." He spun on his heel and left the room quickly, and Riley noted a distinct lack of an "I love you."

Maybe it was just stress, but she was worried it was deliberate.

"What is going on?" Jane asked. "Something is not right."

"It's nothing," Riley mumbled.

"Does it have to do with why you're here?"

She felt her eyes grow wet before she even felt the emotion form. Goddamn it. Why was she crying? Why couldn't she hold this back until she was alone? She'd been able to hide her tears from David when he had fucking cheated on her.

"Are you crying?"

"No," she said, but a tear slipped out.

"Oh, honey, if you're worried he's mad because you're here, don't be. Plenty of people seem angry when they're simply worried."

"It's not that."

"Then what is it?"

She couldn't say it. She didn't want to admit that she was accidentally pregnant, and she didn't think her boyfriend wanted anything to do with it.

"What is it?" Jane repeated. "Is it something serious? Did they run tests and find something?"

"Yeah, kind of. I'm not sick, but I . . ." She still wasn't able to say it. God. Why was this so hard?

"You're what? Anemic? Allergic to something? Oh, what else could they find . . . Pregnant?"

Riley only nodded.

"Pregnant? Really?" Riley braced for the judgment, but Jane's eyes lit up. "That's so exciting!"

"It's not," Riley said. "Oliver doesn't want another kid, so I don't know where we stand on this. I told him he owes me nothing if he doesn't want this one, so I may be doing this on my own."

"You think he would leave you while pregnant?"

"I don't know. Maybe?" Riley shrugged. "It's not like I've had stellar luck with men in my life, and he was *very* against having more. You weren't here when the doctor told me what they found."

"Riley, I doubt he will leave you for anything."

"I don't know," she said. "My head is still killing me, and I've felt so many emotions today that I only want to sleep."

"You're in the first trimester. Exhaustion is very normal."

Riley sighed and she leaned back her head. She wanted answers. She wanted to know if she was doing this alone; but at the same time, she didn't want to get her heart broken if he chose to leave.

"It's going to be okay," her mother reminded her. "I promise."

Oliver

The moment Zoe saw Oliver, she was running to hug him. Her tears hurt him, and he held her tightly.

"Is Mommy okay?"

"Yes, she's okay. She just forgot to eat. Sometimes us adults get so busy we forget our needs."

"I can remind her to eat," Zoe said, wiping at her eyes. "I can do it, like, every minute!"

"I don't think she'll forget again."

Especially now that it's not just her she's eating for.

The thought came unbidden, and it sent a chill down his spine.

Riley was *pregnant*.

Zoe held onto him for what felt like years.

"So, it's nothing serious?" Jack asked much later after Oliver had coaxed Zoe into eating the takeout Jack had ordered.

He shook his head.

"You look like you've seen a ghost," he said, frowning.

He felt like he had. He'd certainly seen the ghost of his own past when the doctor announced Riley was pregnant, and he'd seen the ghost of how she was when he'd fired her, all spitfire and defensiveness.

And that one hurt.

But it wasn't that he blamed her. Emotions were high, and he'd said he didn't want more kids.

However, that first ultrasound changed a lot.

Oliver had never been there for the early days of Zoe's biological mother being pregnant, mostly because she didn't know that she was. When she did find out, she hadn't invited him to ultrasounds. All he got to see was the printed photos afterward.

Hearing the heartbeat and seeing the live imaging was something he couldn't describe. Yes, he was afraid of doing this over again. He'd never realized that seeing his second child, even as small as that, made him ready to do it all over again.

But Riley didn't know that. She thought he was either going to begrudgingly accept responsibility or leave her.

His plan was to do neither.

"It's fine," he said. "Just scary. Thank you for watching Zoe."

"Anytime, son," Jack said. "I ordered enough food for you to east as well. You should have some."

Jack stayed a bit longer, as if waiting for Oliver to elaborate. When he did finally leave, he once again told Oliver he would be there for anything.

He had never been so grateful for his father.

Once Jack was gone, Oliver waited for Riley's return.

Just after ten, the door opened and Riley and Jane walked in.

"Now, be careful on how much coffee you consume, and eat at least *some* fruits and vegetables," Jane was instructing. "And for the love of God, do not skip any more meals."

Riley walked into the living room, rubbing her forehead. She had a bag from a drugstore in her other hand.

"And be sure to take this vita—"

"Mommy!" Zoe yelled, running and launching herself at Riley. She caught the little girl, but both Jane and Oliver jumped up to help.

"It's fine," Riley said, a little irritated. "I can lift what I did before. Mom, you were even there when the doctor told me that."

"Sorry," Jane said, stepping back.

"Are you okay?" Zoe asked.

Riley smiled. Oliver was relieved to see her usual color had returned. He knew she'd eaten at the hospital, but he hoped she'd gotten more since then.

"I'm okay. I'm sorry for scaring you."

"You were asleep and wouldn't wake up! Daddy told me to stay in my room, but I saw you before the ambulance came."

Oliver sighed. He had hoped Zoe would have listened to his order to stay away, but their little girl was just as stubborn as her mother.

"Yeah, that can happen when someone's body is working hard and they forget to eat."

"Want a cookie?" Zoe asked. "Would that make you feel better?"

"That . . . actually does sound good."

"And drink some water," Jane added. Riley sighed and walked to the kitchen.

Jane turned to Oliver, a hesitant smile on her face. "I hear congratulations are in order."

"It seems like it. Sorry I wasn't there for what the doctor said. Is there anything I should be aware of?"

"Not really. All of the usual stuff for pregnant women. Limit caffeine, no ibuprofen, be sure to eat. Hang on." She grabbed her purse and pulled out a pamphlet. "Take this. It lists everything. There are so many new things for pregnant women to avoid."

He took the brochure. His ex hadn't paid much attention to what she should've limited in her diet, and he was surprised to see how long the list was.

Riley returned with a cookie in hand, and Zoe carried a plastic cup of water. Zoe followed her as she sat on the couch and sat next to her.

She hadn't met his eyes yet.

"I'll leave you to talk. I have to get home and somehow explain this all to Amanda without telling her. I'll leave *that* to you."

"Thanks," Riley replied.

"It's no problem. I can imagine why you would want to keep it to yourself after the other night."

Jane left with a smile to both Oliver and Zoe. He stared at the front door, watching Jane leave, wondering how much Riley had told her.

Zoe was attached at Riley's hip while she finished eating the cookie and sipping at the water. Oliver hated delivering the news that she needed to go to sleep, but it was far past her bedtime and he and Riley had a lot to discuss.

As he walked her to her bedroom, he was relieved to see that Zoe's anxiety had lessened. Sleep hit her as soon as she climbed under the blankets, and that left him feeling better about returning to the living room. In the time he was gone, Riley had also fallen asleep, obviously exhausted from her day.

Oliver debated waking her, but he couldn't bring himself to. Instead, he gently picked her up and carried her to their bedroom.

He stayed up much later, content to focus on this new information. Armed with the knowledge of a baby, and having a padded bank account, he turned to his phone. He didn't usually shop. When he did, it was for his suits for work or something for the house.

But things had changed, and Riley would have to get over her aversion to the idea of being spoiled. Because she and their child certainly would be.

He focused on making Riley's life easier, and ordered everything he wanted for their future child.

Riley

Riley awoke to the doorbell ringing.

She blearily opened her eyes, the exhaustion of the day before still weighing her down. She'd slept in, and the time on her phone told her it was almost noon. Next to her, Oliver was asleep. His hand was on her hip, which was at least some kind of sign he didn't hate her.

Her heart jolted with the idea that everything could turn out all right, but she shook it away. She didn't want to hope for the best and get the worst.

The doorbell rang again and carefully, she got up, not wanting him to be disturbed.

What she saw on the front porch was shocking.

A disgruntled delivery man tapped his foot impatiently, pushing his tablet at her. Thrown for a loop, she signed without thinking. When the man stomped off, Riley saw exactly *why* he was mad.

There were boxes everywhere. So many that she thought this must be a mistake, but when she checked the delivery address, Oliver's name was on every single one of them.

Had he been hacked?

No, the packages wouldn't have been delivered to the house then.

Riley had no idea how she would get it all inside, but lucky for her, there was a very excited five-year-old who'd just joined her downstairs.

"Mommy?"

"Zoe?" Riley said, instant panic in her voice thinking she and Oliver had just left their daughter alone in the house all morning. "How long have you been up?"

"For a bit. I played with my dolls so you and Daddy could sleep in."

For the first time, Riley took in the state of the living room. Toys were everywhere from Zoe's attempt to entertain herself.

But that was a problem for the future.

"What are all these boxes?" Zoe asked.

"I-I don't know," Riley said. "Can you help me carry them in?"

Zoe eagerly nodded and Riley wondered if Oliver had decided to replace every single one of her toys.

Together, they managed to get all the smaller boxes. A few of them felt way too heavy for Riley to lift comfortably.

The movement must have woken up Oliver because he walked around the corner as Riley set down the last box she could carry.

"Riley," Oliver said, his voice tight. "You shouldn't be lifting—"

"The doctor said I could lift what I was before, remember?" Riley said. "And I should be asking the questions here. What is all this?"

"Stuff."

"Stuff for what?"

Oliver glanced at Zoe, and Riley sighed when she realized that, whatever it was, would have to wait until she wasn't in the room.

"Is any of it for me?" Zoe asked, eyes bright.

"Hang on," Oliver said, surveying the items. "This one is."

This box had the same shipping label as the rest, but clearly showed a huge dollhouse on the side.

"The whole box?" Zoe said, jaw dropping.

"Yep, the whole box." Oliver grabbed scissors and opened it for her. He pulled out the pink plastic folding dollhouse and the assortment of dolls it came with.

"Yes!" Zoe squealed as she dragged the new toy across the room to play with.

"I guess it was a good idea to pay for the faster delivery for that item," Oliver said, smiling in the direction of his daughter. "Aren't you glad we live right next to a distribution hub for most of this?"

"I still don't know what all of this is," Riley muttered, shoulders tense.

"Just some stuff for the baby."

"What? You bought *all* of this for the baby?"

He shrugged. "I wanted to."

For a short, terrifying moment, Riley wondered if this was his parting gift. Maybe he'd offer to give her everything she needed before dumping her. The thought brought tears to her eyes, but she blinked them away.

"Riley," Oliver started, walking over to her.

"Why?" she asked, hating the way her voice cracked on the words.

"You should eat."

"You should tell me what's going on."

"I will," he said. "But you're still recovering, and I'm not letting what happened yesterday happen again."

She knew he was right. She sighed and walked to the kitchen. When she opened the refrigerator door, she found it fully stocked with . . . everything she loved.

"What the—"

"Surprise. I went to the store. Did you know there's one store in Nashville that's twenty-four hours?"

"This is hundreds of dollars of stuff."

"Yeah, and if you mention paying me back, I'll order more."

"Is this your way of dumping me?" she snapped, turning to him. "Spoil me and say you don't want this kid?"

She regretted it the moment it left her lips. Some of the easiness in his features tightened. She prepared herself for him to snap right back at her.

"Riley," he said slowly. "Do you really think that?"

"I don't know what to think," she said. "The last time we talked, we were discussing . . ." She lowered her voice. "If you even wanted this."

"Of course I want this."

"The last time we talked about kids, you said you didn't."

"And then I saw the ultrasound."

Her heart jolted again, and it hit her that things might not go wrong this time. Maybe there was no sad ending.

"I don't want to trap you," she said, her voice thick with emotion.

"This was just as big of a shock to you as it was me," he said. "If your plans can change so quickly, why can't mine?"

She looked away.

People before him never bent for her. They expected her to be the flexible one and she did it until she broke.

She expected things to end badly because it was all she'd ever known.

"So . . . all this is for the baby?" she asked.

Oliver laughed. "No. I did some research for what pregnant women need. About half of it is for you. It's maternity clothes, body pillows, anything the Internet said you might need."

"How much did you spend?"

"I'm not going to answer that."

"Maybe I should cover some of it."

"That's strike one," he said, smiling at her. "Now I'm going to find something else you need."

"What?"

"Every time you offer to pay for the *gift* I get you, I'm going to order you something else. I know you, Riley. You respond better to action sometimes. All of these are gifts. I'm not secretly angry or expecting anything in return. Let me treat you for once."

And Oliver had no pinched brow or frown in his expression. She couldn't hear a hint of secret resentment in his voice, just like when he had bought her something in the past.

She glanced out across the living room. Her first instinct was to believe this came with conditions—that one day, this would bite her in the ass.

But this was Oliver, and he was different than everyone else.

"Can I . . . can I tell you what shoes I actually want?"

Oliver's eyes widened. "Seriously?"

"There's this brand I've been looking at for six months," she admitted. "I could never justify them."

"Tell me them now then," he said. "Before you change your mind."

She did, even though her voice shook as she said it.

She was scared, but she trusted him.

And she had to admit, maybe Kyla was right. There *was* some benefit to having a rich boyfriend.

Oliver moved fast in ordering the shoes. He'd been right to, because she opened her mouth to take it back right as he hit order.

"Nope," he said upon seeing her expression. "No returns."

Her eyes grew wet, her emotions finally taking over.

"Thank you," she said, her heart racing at the idea of letting him *finally* do things for her.

"I'm with you through anything," he said, walking up to her. He set his hands on either side of her cheeks and she leaned into the gesture. "This wasn't what I planned, but there was no question when I heard their heartbeat and saw them for the first time. If you didn't want them, then I'd do it all like I did with Zoe."

"But I do want them," she said, tearfully. "I really do."

"Then let's do this together. All of it. Even the tough parts."

Riley nodded, eyes shining with unshed tears.

"How far along are you?"

"The doctor said I looked to be almost two months, give or take a few weeks."

"That far?"

"I wasn't taking my birth control regularly before we switched to condoms. After that one night in the shower, I figured I could take a Plan B pill but . . . I got distracted trying to find it."

"It's fine. This could have happened even if you had been taking it regularly. Sex comes with this possibility. I've always known that."

"I was so afraid you were going to blame me."

"No," he said firmly. "We're in this together. I wouldn't leave because something unexpected happened. I wish you hadn't thought that, but I understand why."

"I have so much to work on in therapy," Riley said.

"I'm with you through anything. I can promise you that."

"Is that why you were looking at rings?" She planned on keeping that knowledge to herself, but she couldn't help it after what he'd said.

"Wait, what?" he asked. "How did you know?"

"I found the brochure the day I planned to take the Plan B," Riley said, laughing. "That was the distraction."

"I'm still planning a nice proposal. Pretend you didn't see anything."

"Fine. But you do know my answer is yes, right?"

Relief hit Oliver. "I do."

She smiled. "Good. So we're together forever?"

"Under any conditions," he replied, planting a long, loving kiss on her lips.

Riley took the day off work. While she knew she needed to tell Camilla, she also wanted to go through the piles of boxes in their living room first and see what Oliver had purchased.

Her mother reached out not too long after they were all up to offer to take Zoe out for lunch to give Riley and Oliver some more alone time. They waited until Zoe was at lunch with her Gran to open up everything.

And damn, Oliver had good taste. The body pillow he bought was going to be her best friend once the infamous aches and pains of later pregnancy started. The clothes he'd gotten made her cry again.

Instead of dresses or fancy shirts she'd never wear, he picked out basics. Maternity T-shirts and comfortable pants.

Plus, a whole box of plus-sized flannels in case she gained weight.

And he'd looked like a kid on Christmas the entire time, even though *she* was the one getting spoiled.

She made sure to hug him for a full minute, still resisting the urge to insist she pay him back.

"How did you even get all of this here in one night anyway?"

"Lots of places have one-day shipping," he said, smiling. "But more is on the way."

Riley laughed, both hoping and not hoping he was serious.

She was starting to feel a bit hungry and he fixed her favorite meal. While he was in the kitchen, she heard a knock at the door.

She slowly walked to it, thinking it was more boxes, but blinked in confusion when she saw her sister. Amanda looked harried, and she wondered if she was going to hear some sort of bad news about Amanda's life.

"What happened?" Amanda asked, sounding worried. "I got a call from the hospital last night saying you *passed out*, and mom comes back lying and telling me everything is fine. You haven't answered your phone in hours, and you do *not* look okay."

Oh. Amanda was here for *her*.

"I'm fine. I passed out because I didn't eat all day."

"No. No way. There has to be more going on."

There *was* more going on, but she wasn't sure what she should say. Amanda didn't announce until week twelve, and Riley hadn't even begun making these decisions for herself.

"I was so scared," Amanda said, her eyes wet. "I was scared that the last time I saw you was going to be me being a total bitch to you because of my own problems! How could I let that happen?"

She wasn't sure what to say, and now because Amanda was crying, she wanted to as well.

"I am so sorry," Amanda said, pulling Riley into a tight hug. "I shouldn't have ever compared you to me. You and Oliver are so perfect together and I was so selfish to make it about me. You deserve better. I'm going to start therapy and I'm going to talk to someone about what's happened, because you deserve a better sister than I've ever been."

"I-I forgive you," Riley stuttered. Her mind worked to try and make sense of Amanda *apologizing*. She figured they would do what they always did: avoid each other for a few weeks and then pretend it never happened when Jane inevitably invited them over for a family get together.

"Oliver said you would, but I know I wouldn't if I were you, and what does that say about me?" Amanda sobbed. "I am so sorry."

"It's okay," Riley reassured her. "Even if I'm angry, we can work on it. If we're both trying to be better, then it's going to work out."

"How are you so nice?" Amanda asked. "You've had so many terrible things happen to you, and I'm one of them."

"I . . . it's not all bad. I have Zoe and Oliver."

Amanda nodded. Her tears finally subsided, and Riley wiped at her eyes, glad she didn't completely lose it.

"Thank you," Amanda said. "I'm going to be better. I promise."

"Good," Riley said. "That's all I ask."

"You never said why you passed out." Amanda was frowning as she pulled away. "Was it really because you forgot to eat?"

"No," Riley admitted with a sigh. "It's not anything serious, but they did find something."

Amanda raised her eyebrows.

"I'm . . . I'm pregnant."

Her jaw dropped. She was glad she was able to say it today. Hearing that Oliver wasn't mad at her and was in this with her made it so much easier to accept.

"Holy shit. Oliver is gonna be dad. Again! Was it planned?"

Riley shook her head. "Birth control issues."

"How far along are you?" she asked excitedly.

"Um, somewhere around two months? Further along than I thought."

"Then the exhaustion has gotten you," Amanda said. "When I was pregnant, the first trimester was a blur. There's a really good supplement I tried with my second pregnancy that saved me. Hang on, I'll pull it up."

Amanda and Riley talked details for a while. Amanda had been pregnant more recently and knew the best hospital and delivery doctors for Riley to go to. Her sister didn't show one ounce of jealousy, and she was relieved that they were hopefully going to be on the same page for once.

"What are all the boxes for?"

"Oh, um, Oliver went a little wild last night."

"This is all for the baby?"

"And some for me and Zoe." Riley bit her lip, worried Amanda's jealousy would finally show.

"Wow," Amanda said. "This is amazing. It's what you deserve."

"You're not . . . upset?"

"I mean, I wish James had done even a fraction of this." She gestured around the mess of the house. "But that isn't your fault. I *am* happy for you. Truly."

"Thank you," Riley said, hugging her.

"Amanda?" Oliver asked, coming into the room. Riley's attention was on him and the delicious smelling cinnamon rolls he had on a plate in his hands.

"Hi, Oliver," Amanda said. "I had to come check on Riley. I knew mom's excuse was a lie."

Oliver glanced at Riley, as if asking how much she knew.

"I told her," Riley admitted. "But I think she'd figure it out given the amount of baby stuff scattered all over the place."

"I'm so happy for you both. Congratulations." Amanda sounded so genuine, and it made emotion well up in Riley's throat. "Aw, don't cry. Although I know there's not much you can do. The Emerson women always cry while pregnant. And after. The tears never really stop. Maybe I can ask my new therapist if that's some kind of hereditary thing."

"You've got a therapist already?" Riley asked.

"I've called a couple offices trying to find one. I know it's going to be hard working on myself," she admitted. "But I won't regret it."

"I don't think I will, either."

Amanda stayed for an hour, offering tips for what to expect. After that, Riley and Oliver busied themselves with putting together baby things.

While this wasn't what she planned, Riley couldn't help but be excited for the future. And now that she knew Oliver was too, it made it all the better.

Chapter Sixteen

Two Months Later

Riley

After so long with no ring, Riley was beginning to wonder if she'd imagined finding that pamphlet in Oliver's drawer.

It was Christmastime once again. She was sporting a small bump that looked more like she was perpetually bloated than she was pregnant. Oliver had been there for every doctor's appointment and made sure to check on her at least twice a day.

He'd told her that he missed all of this with Zoe, and he was just as new to it as she was. He had been so kind and gentle with her through the pregnancy hormones. She couldn't imagine going through any of it with anyone else.

They'd told Zoe about the baby a week ago. Since then, the little girl had been more than excited about it. She was looking forward to being a big sister so much so that she had been learning how to take care of a baby to be able to "help" after they were born.

At the first ultrasound where they could tell the gender, the baby was being stubborn about it, which led Riley to decide she didn't want to know until they were born. It was more fun to guess.

She had a strong inclination it was a boy. Oliver seemed certain it was a girl. Zoe didn't care either way, but she did say her favorite color was blue.

Riley was taking to pregnancy well. She'd cut back on her managing hours, but worked more on a third location that she Camilla were planning. This additional spot meant far more administrative work needed to be done, so she was able to do that and still earn her salary. Oliver had mentioned she could quit her job if she needed, and she knew Camilla would understand, but she honestly enjoyed working. If she ever felt differently in the future, then it was nice to know there were other options.

The chilly nights of December were back when Riley, Oliver, and Zoe found themselves back at the Nashville botanical garden for the light displays, but this time Amanda, Luke, and Landon had tagged along. Once both sisters agreed to go, Jane wanted to, as well. Then, somehow, Camilla tagged along, stating she wanted to be part of the family.

Riley never thought such a big group of the Emerson clan plus Camilla could go well, but ever since Amanda had started therapy, she was much more reasonable. Her mother was too.

While the kids played in the field, the adults huddled together to catch up. It was the first family event that had no tears or drama—just good conversation.

The lights in the dark of the early night, coupled with the steaming cups of hot chocolate Oliver had gotten all of them, made for a picturesque scene. Eventually, the kids began to move on, and the group of cold adults followed.

Eventually, they arrived at the mansion in the gardens, a historical building repurposed into a museum. The kids wanted to take pictures with Santa, and while Zoe and Landon were making funny faces behind Luke and Santa, Riley was snapping photos.

Oliver stood next to her, a warm hand on her back as they watched their little family enjoy the night.

After Santa, they all went through the gardens and found a beautiful arch where people were posing for photos. Riley noticed both Jane and Camilla getting their phones out, but she thought it was because of the beautiful scenery.

She turned to find Oliver on one knee.

"Riley," he started, "I am in awe of you, your selflessness when adopting Zoe, the beauty of your smile and how it lights up even the darkest of my days, your sense of humor, and how you are always yourself, even when others disagree. A part of me fell for you the moment you walked through my door, but you endlessly find ways to make me love you more. It would be my greatest honor to have you as my wife. Will you marry me?"

What he held was a ring Riley had always wanted. The family heirloom, her grandmother's, one she thought was either given to Amanda or lost. It was a simple band with a single perfectly cut diamond in the center; she'd studied it for years in hopes she would someday get it.

She had an inkling this was coming, but the tears fell freely anyway. This was a perfect scene, and they were surrounded by everyone in her family. Two years ago, this was all a pipe dream, and now she had the man of her dreams, and they were going to get married.

It was amazing how things could change so quickly.

"Yes!" she exclaimed, tears running down her cheeks. Oliver slid the ring onto her finger and she spent a long moment marveling at how it fit and how it shined like new despite being an old family heirloom. It was perfect in every way.

Just like them.

By the time they were ready to head home, Zoe declared she was staying at Gran's.

When Riley, still emotional from the engagement, raised an eyebrow at her mother, Jane only shrugged. "Enjoy your alone time, Riley. Especially before the baby. I'll watch Zoe for the night."

"Wow," Amanda said. "Where was this attitude when I was with James?"

"I would have liked to see James watch his own kids for a change," Jane said. "Maybe the better man you date next will meet my very low standards."

"Wait," Amanda said. "I shouldn't have brought myself into such an amazing day for Riley. Sorry." And to her credit, she did look sheepish.

She still slipped up, but she'd done a lot of growing in therapy.

Riley smiled and thanked her.

Oliver started to pull her away, and after they both said their goodbyes to Zoe, he drove them home.

"So, was it to your standards?" he asked. "I mean, you knew it was coming, but I hope you were at least a little surprised."

"Were the tears not enough?" she said, laughing. "Yes, it was perfect. I loved it."

"Well, I love *you*, so I wanted it to be."

Riley smiled over at him, fingers moving to play with her new ring. When she was a kid, she'd wore it to pretend she was married, and it still felt familiar to her.

"Thank you for getting this ring. It's perfect."

"It's the only thing that suits you." His voice was soft and gentle.

God, she loved this man.

When they pulled into the driveway, he turned to her. "Now, do you remember our agreement . . ."

Her face flushed as she remembered what she'd said a month ago when she was growing impatient to get proposed to.

If you propose, I'll let you make me cum as many times as you can.

"I do," she said. Her heart raced in anticipation.

"Let's go inside."

They didn't make it very far. The moment the door shut, he was kissing her, pressing her against the frame.

Her body heated, and all she could think about was if he would make true on the promise. She figured they wouldn't make it to the bedroom, but he picked her up. Riley yelped in shock, but she'd grown to realize he would never drop her.

"We're doing this in the bed," he said, his voice gruff. He laid her down, pulling her sweater off her immediately. The cool air hit her skin, making her erupt into goose bumps.

But the warmth of Oliver's body calmed those as his skin met hers. For a long time, they only kissed, his hand trailing downwards, tracing the skin of her side and hip, before they dipped under her waistband of her soft leggings.

When his hand touched her, it was a gentle movement, but her body was worked up in excited anticipation, so he met wetness. These days, she knew better than to feel insecurity about her body.

Oliver's mouth moved to her ear. "I love it when you feel like this."

She flushed, and the heat in her body only made his hand's actions do more to her. He knew exactly what she liked, and she found that her body responded to him quickly.

As her orgasm climbed, her moans did too. When she finally peaked, she let out a cry and jerked against him.

Breathlessly, as her brain came back online, she had to resist the urge to say it was her turn to focus on him. He made her feel *so* good, and she wanted to return the favor.

"We're focusing on you," he said, kissing her neck. She dimly wondered if he was a mind reader. He took a moment to kiss her breasts and chest, but then he arrived at her core, which was still worked up from her first orgasm.

But he was gentle. When his tongue ran over her clit, the light pressure was exactly what she needed. She ran her hands through his hair, moving her hips in time with his strokes.

When she came again, her body convulsed. She couldn't remember if she made a noise or not, but all she could do was ride the wave of something new, something different.

After the pleasure finally ebbed, she looked down to see him watching her intently. She blushed and opened her mouth to ask if it was finally his turn.

He only shook his head and said it was nowhere near over.

After that, she lost count of how many times she came. Oliver was patient, but unrelenting. She didn't even know she could feel this way, and even more strangely, he seemed to take pleasure in hers. Time passed, lost in a haze of heat and moans, and when he finally pushed into her, hours later, she was lost somewhere in the stars.

"I can't wait to marry you," she said breathlessly as he thrust inside.

"I've been thinking the same thing for a long time."

Oliver

The reality of planning a wedding when a baby was on the way was challenging. They had two choices: have a huge wedding after the baby was born and deal with wedding planning on top of a newborn, or try to rush to get married before they had the baby.

Riley was content to wait, but Oliver remembered how challenging newborn Zoe had been, and he worried they would never actually plan the wedding if they were too busy being new parents.

"Then maybe we should just get married at the courthouse," she told him. "Do something small and if we have time after the baby gets here, we can do something bigger."

"That's probably our best option," he'd muttered, even though he wasn't exactly thrilled with it.

He didn't know why he was surprised when she cornered him a week later, insisting they get moving on the marriage certificate sooner rather than later.

Then again, since she was pregnant, she was in the mood to get stuff done rather than wait.

They didn't tell very many people, but once Jane found out, she insisted she come. Then Jack did the same, and suddenly, they had a whole crowd. Oliver suggested they do it at the Opryland Resort in the middle of the day instead for more space.

It was Riley's dream wedding venue, after all.

"So we're having a wedding," Riley said as they saw their guest list grow.

"Yes, but it'll be small," he replied. "And it's indoors. We don't have to worry about the weather."

"Then I guess a wedding we'll have," she said. "I wonder if Camilla is good at this stuff."

It turned out Camilla was *not* good at party planning, but Vanessa was. Once she heard about nuptials, she stepped in and offered to plan the whole thing, and she did it so well that Oliver suggested this should be her job instead of being a middle school teacher.

They scored space at one of the prime wedding spots at the resort grounds and rented one of the small reception areas on the property.

Riley was able to find a dress in a few days; she got a great deal on one in stock that they would alter for her. At first, she'd been embarrassed about the baby bump being in the gown. Then she'd proclaimed she was tired of society's expectations regarding when women should get pregnant and decided to flaunt it.

Their wedding was presided over by an officiant Oliver hired who encouraged them to write their own vows.

Zoe declared herself the flower girl. They asked Luke to be the ring bearer, and Landon offered to be the photographer. The real photographer, someone Oliver had also hired, was very amused at Landon's attempt to upstage him.

The wedding day was simple and elegant. They were surrounded by a beautiful landscape and all of their loved ones. With Jack on her arm, proudly stepping in where her own father never wanted to, Riley walked down the aisle in a long, clean, white dress holding eucalyptus and pink flowers. Zoe walked in front of her, throwing rose petals at everyone she saw.

Oliver didn't think he would ever cry at his own wedding, but he felt tears wet his cheeks when he saw Riley.

"You look beautiful," he said the moment his hand met hers.

A tear slipped from Riley's eye, and she'd later tell him she opted for very quality waterproof makeup. Nothing smeared even as more tears fell.

Oliver barely listened to the officiant because he was too busy looking at the love of his life. He stared at her longingly, wanting to commit her to memory in this moment.

When he got to his vows, he almost forgot them.

"Riley," he started, "I wish words could express how much I love you." Her face was painted over in light makeup, and he would bet she was blushing underneath it. "But I'll try my best to. I vow to love you through everything, your good days, your bad ones, and especially the awful ones. I vow to always choose you, even when we argue, because you are the greatest choice I could ever make. Without you, I am only a shell of myself, and since I've known you, I've become complete. I vow never to forget how much you mean to me, and always be by your side, no matter what obstacles we may face."

She wiped away her stray tears and smiled. "I don't know if mine measure up," she whispered.

"I'm sure they will."

"Okay, here goes," she said as she wiped another tear with the back of her hand. "Oliver, I never imagined I would have a love so profound as yours, and now that I have it, I vow to never let it go. You're my person, my best friend, my first real love, and I will always cherish that. I vow to always care about you, even in our difficult moments, because you mean more to me than any conflict ever could. I vow to love you and our daughter and our new child to the ends of the earth."

"You already do," he said.

"Well, I always will," she replied, smiling wetly.

He kissed her before their official "I do" because he couldn't be bothered to wait any longer.

It was bliss.

Epilogue

Riley

The thing about being pregnant past forty weeks was: it sucked.

Everyone kept looking at her like she would jump into labor at any moment, and Riley was more than tired of being looked at like a balloon that was about to explode.

It was the beginning of summer, and while she had been lucky to miss out on the worst of the heat as the baby grew, the temperature had been steadily climbing, and she was the biggest she was going to get.

She was more than ready to be done with it.

She hadn't done much thinking about the birth, but she knew it wasn't going to be a pleasant experience. There was a rough outline of a birth plan, but her being overdue meant her doctor was very close to inducing her, which put the inevitability of it all right in front of her.

Oliver had been more than attentive throughout her entire pregnancy, and while she was so grateful for the attention, sometimes she wanted to be alone in the peace and quiet of an empty home.

As the weeks sped by leading up to her due date, Riley had reduced her hours even further. Both Oliver and Camilla insisted that she stop entirely, thinking that the long hours on her feet weren't good for her, but her doctor had fortunately come to her aid and said everything was fine as long as she took it easy.

Riley was still salary, but her responsibilities were more back of office than anything. She dove into marketing and

HR work that she'd never done before, but it kept her busy. Most of the time she worked in the guest room, which they had been slowly converting to a nursery.

She couldn't wait to be back in the shop more, though.

This was one of those morning where it was just her and Zoe. It had been hectic, with Zoe asking a hundred and one questions about the baby, but she had been understanding when Riley asked if she could have a moment to herself. Riley sometimes found she needed the stillness to process her daily emotions.

Sally would be proud.

For most of the morning, she had been feeling an uncomfortable twinge in her stomach. She knew these were probably Braxton-Hicks contractions, which weren't *real* contractions, but she also knew if she told Oliver, he would be rushing her to the hospital way before she was ready. They'd already gone once, only to find out she was not in labor, much to her dismay.

Her doctor had given her until their next appointment, which was tomorrow, to see if she would go into labor on her own. If not, they would induce her that day. At this point, she was making peace with the fact that she would be induced.

She was expecting a normal day. She figured she could hang out with Zoe and watch movies until Oliver got home.

The slight pain in her stomach only came once in a while, but it persisted.

Oliver was at work, ensuring that he would be good to be off for a month once the baby arrived. Riley had told him to go, insisting she would be fine.

And she was fine.

Until she wasn't.

After a few hours of these pains, she started timing them. They were relatively consistent, but growing more and more intense.

As they neared ten minutes apart, she began to suspect this was the real deal.

Oliver wasn't due home until five, but Zoe proved to be enough of a distraction for Riley to ignore the pain and get through her day. The pains she was feeling weren't bad enough to stop her mid-speech, so she doubted Zoe noticed anything.

As the day progressed, Riley continued timing her contractions, but she missed a few here and there while Zoe rambled and helped her with dinner.

By the time Oliver got home, she was wincing when each one hit.

He, of course, picked up on it immediately.

"Are you okay?"

"I'm fine. Just . . . maybe contracting."

His eyes widened.

"I don't know if it's the real thing. My doctor said I wasn't showing any progress toward—"

If Riley hadn't looked it up in preparation for labor, she probably would have thought she'd peed herself. Her leggings were damp and once the water started, it wouldn't stop.

"What?" Oliver asked, eyes trained her expression.

"I think my water broke."

Oliver's eyes trailed down, as if he was expected a puddle.

"No, it's not gonna be like in the movies—" She stopped mid-sentence, wincing as a particularly powerful contraction hit her.

He dropped his bag and immediately called Jane to coordinate childcare.

Riley missed most of the conversation. All she could feel was the *pain* of the contraction. They were definitely no longer tolerable.

"I'm calling the doula, and Jane is on her way," he said, coming back into the room.

Her mother arrived within minutes, making Riley wonder how many laws she broke to get to Oliver's house so quickly, and he pushed her out the door with a firm hand on her back.

Her contractions came faster than she would have like, and she was wet and in agony. While Zoe was present, it was her goal to appear okay, because the last thing her daughter needed was to see her in pain.

All bets were off when they got to the car.

"Holy motherfucking hell, this hurts!"

Oliver sped out of the driveway. "I know, but hopefully we can get to the hospital where they can get you an epidural immediately."

She groaned, which turned guttural when another contraction hit her. The pain was so intense it felt like it was all she could focus on. Her sense of humor was gone. She couldn't find any joy. It was all about survival.

He must have sped to the hospital because they were there in minutes. She was immediately plopped into a wheelchair and taken to a room.

"I don't think I can do this," she said, panic in her voice. "This is too much."

"You can do it," Oliver said. "If there's anyone who can, it's you."

"Oh God, fuck this. I never want kids *again*."

A nurse came in wearing gloves and a smile. "Okay, momma," she said in a southern drawl. "Let's check ya."

Riley didn't want anyone *near* her, but she figured this was part of giving birth, so she kept her complaints to herself.

The nurse continued smiling and did her business, but her cheer paled quickly. "Oh my, it's time to push."

"What!" Riley and Oliver yelled.

She had never seen people file into a room so fast. Suddenly, she was moved from a triage area to an actual room, and a doctor was running in.

She didn't remember much about the pushing, only that Oliver held her hands tightly, and she *hated* every second of it. She didn't know how much time had passed, but then it was over, and there was a new baby in her arms.

"It's a boy!" the doctor announced.

Riley was crying, but she managed to say, "I fucking knew it."

Oliver had tears in his eyes too. "I've never been happier to be wrong," he said as he planted a kiss on her forehead.

They named their child Xavier Jack Brian, and three became four.

Oliver

Having a baby was not easy.

But it was easier doing it with someone you loved.

Xavier was a completely different child than Zoe. He was calmer and had a strong bond with Riley.

She had chosen breastfeeding, and luckily, she seemed well suited to it. Oliver was so used to having to prep bottles for Zoe that he wasn't sure what to do with himself now that she handled most of the feedings.

He offered to take on the nighttime diaper changes.

Riley was taking to parenting as well as she had with Zoe. She had struggled with some of it, especially the exhaustion, but she hadn't snapped at him or Zoe once. She'd only cried once when she wanted pizza and Xavier was wailing for food himself.

She figured out how to eat with one hand very quickly.

Zoe loved her little brother and constantly asked to hold him. When Riley was feeding him, Zoe would get her own dolls and pretended to be mommy to them. Oliver knew she was going to take good care of him.

He tried to help as much as he could, but he couldn't keep his job at bay for much longer. Eventually, after extending to a month and a half off, he returned to work, which was unfortunately still during summer break for Zoe. Jane took the day off, but Riley said she wanted to see if she could handle both kids on her own. Jane remained on standby in case she got overwhelmed, which made Oliver feel better about returning to the office.

When he got in, he knew it was going to be a long one.

And for a father of two, long days were harder than they used to be. All he wanted was to be home with Riley, Zoe, and Xavier, but he also had to work.

His day went by painfully slowly, and the sun had sunk low in the sky by the time he put his laptop away. Riley hadn't messaged all day. It worried him and he hated how late he'd stayed in a near-useless attempt to catch up on work.

When he got home, he noticed Jane's car wasn't in the driveway, and he mentally prepared himself for a disaster zone. He trusted Riley, and knew she would do her best, but there had been no reprieve when it came to baby Zoe, and Oliver could still remember the sleepless nights.

But he walked into a quiet house.

The TV was playing *Frozen* and Zoe's dolls were all around the house, but everything was . . . *peaceful.*

Oliver walked to her room and found her fast asleep on her bed. She had her favorite ugly doll lying next to her. He smiled at his daughter before heading back downstairs to check on Riley next.

She was in the master bedroom, looking at her laptop. Xavier was asleep in his bassinet beside her.

"You got both kids to bed?" he asked, shocked.

She jumped. "God, don't sneak up on me like that."

"Sorry," he said. "I just expected today to be . . . worse."

"It was hard," she said, sighing. "Zoe had to learn the art of patience, but I made it work. The house is a total wreck though . . ."

"It reminds me of your first night," he said softly. "When you got Zoe to bed for the first time without me."

"Oh, yeah," she said, smiling. "That night was a dumpster fire too, but they're asleep now. That's what matters."

He kissed her. "You did great."

"Say that to the pile of toys in the living room."

"I've got it," he said. "Have I ever told you I'm so happy I have you?"

She blushed, and that familiar look of panic never crossed her face. She had gotten so much better about compliments. "You have. Once or twice."

"I'll tell you every day until we're old," he said. "I love you."

"I love you too. And I hate to spoil the moment, but I'd love some of that leftover taco casserole in the fridge."

"I'll get it for you," he told her, kissing her forehead.

This was nothing like how things had been when Zoe was little. He wasn't alone. He wasn't lonely. He felt complete. They had their little family in their home, and he couldn't imagine wanting anything else.

And it was all because of the woman in the other room.

He smiled and got her the food she needed before he settled in for the night. It hadn't been easy getting here, but he couldn't regret one moment of it.

And he couldn't wait to see what came next.

Acknowledgments

Thank you to everyone who's read and enjoyed Oliver and Riley's story. Your support means so much. Also, to my editor, Kasey, I thank you so much for your help with these manuscripts. Your edits and suggestions make me a better writer.

To Josh, thank you for watching our son and supporting me while I write. I could never ask for a better partner than you. And Cass and Lizzie, thank you for supporting me and reading my work before it is published. Having friends who are with me every step of the way has changed my life. I owe you two a lot.

About the Author

Elle Rivers lives in Tennessee with her husband, son, seven cats, and four chickens. When not writing, she can be found reading, staring at her pets, or playing with her kiddo. She can be found on Twitter and Instagram as @elleswrites and on Tiktok as @AuthorElleRivers and @ElleRiversAuthor.

Made in the USA
Columbia, SC
30 August 2023

22235439R00120